W9-BYH-453

the
River
road

DEMCO

the River road

a Novel in Stories

Tricia Currans-Sheehan

The publication of *The River Road: A Novel in Stories* is made possible by the generous support of the McKnight Foundation and other contributors to New Rivers Press.

For academic permission please contact Frederick T. Courtright at 570-839-7477 or permdude@eclipse.net. For all other permissions, contact The Copyright Clearance Center at 978-750-8400 or info@copyright.com.

New Rivers Press is a nonprofit literary press associated with Minnesota State University Moorhead.

Wayne Gudmundson, Director
Alan Davis, Senior Editor
Donna Carlson, Managing Editor
Thom Tammaro, Poetry Editor
Kevin Carollo, MVP Poetry Coordinator
Liz Severn, MVP Fiction Coordinator

Publishing Intern: Jennifer Bakken
Honors Apprentice: Amanda Reiser
The River Road: A Novel in Stories Book Team: Janet Aarness, Susan Flipp,
        Brittany Mathiason, Rachel Roe
Editorial Interns: Janet Aarness, Ann Rosenquist Fee, Susan Flipp,
        Chris Hingley, Amanda Huggett, Steve Lauder, Brittany
        Mathiason, Kellie Meehlhause, Ellie Musselman, Rachel Roe,
        Kristen Underdahl
Design Interns: Danielle DeKruif, Alison Eickhoff, Angelina Lennington,
        Kristen Stalboerger, Stephanie Thomas
Festival Coordinator: Heather Steinmann
Allen Sheets, Design Manager
Deb Hval, Business Manager

Printed in the United States of America.

New Rivers Press
c/o MSUM
1104 7th Avenue South
Moorhead, MN 56563
www.newriverspress.com

I dedicate this novel in stories to my mother, Salome Antoine Currans.

Table of contents

the Last trapshoot

1957

Once a year on a Sunday in October before the corn was picked, I used to go to a trapshoot in Billy Foy's pasture across from his house on the river road. I would race there, taking a shortcut through our pasture. My dad didn't go. He said it was stupid to waste those bullets on fake birds; you should save them for killing deer or rabid raccoons or, like the pioneers, for chasing that renegade Inkpaduta out of the river bottom.

But one Sunday it all ended. It was chilly that morning but the sun warmed things up later on. The sheep pasture had clumps of dried grasses and weeds sticking up high with seeds ready to spill out. The sheep had been taken to another field two weeks earlier, and Billy had mowed where people would be parking and walking.

Most of the hunters were farmers, some in overalls, who wanted to show off their prized shotguns. They drove up in their pickups, a few bringing along their hunting dogs and wives and kids. About fifty feet from the clubhouse, Billy had pounded in the ground a handwritten sign on a stick that said *Parking Starts Here*. He wanted to leave an open space in front of the clubhouse door so there was

room to mill around. All along the field lane were pickups that
had been recently hosed down for the event. Most of the hunters
carried their guns in drab green canvas cases and a few didn't bother.
They held the butt in their palm with the stalk leaning against their
shoulder. They hurried toward the clubhouse where the other hunters
stood around joking about how well they planned to shoot clay
birdies out of the sky. The man who shot most of the ten clay pigeons
was the winner for that round, and then he advanced to another
round. By the end of the afternoon only five hunters would be lined
up facing the open pasture with a trap house hidden like a bunker out
in front of them.

The green trap house sat buried in the ground, only a foot of roof
exposed. The trap setter had to crawl into the bunker, which was three
feet high. The hunter who was waiting for the pigeon would call out,
"Pull!" and the boy running the trap, usually one of my cousins, would
eject it, aiming the thing in a different direction each time. The hunter
had to quickly follow the flying pigeon, aim, and fire at it before it
got too low to the ground. Billy always worried that some young pup
would try to shoot when it got too low and would hit the bunker. The
bunker was made of wood with sheet-metal siding painted dark green
to blend in with the grasses. If you looked closely, the sheet metal had
lots of holes in it from the spray of the shotgun shells.

But this Sunday a maroon Cadillac with a Michigan license plate
pulled into the field and drove right up to the first pickup that started
the lineup and this car edged alongside, knocking down Billy's sign
to be first in line. Two people got out—a man and a woman. But this
woman wasn't going to serve loose meat Maid Rite sandwiches. No,
sirree, she was going to shoot. She wore a safari outfit—tan pants and
jacket with lots of pockets—and she had on brown leather boots with
thick two-inch heels. Under the jacket there was a red turtleneck. She
was taller than most of the men out there. Her hair was blonde like
the silk on an ear of corn. It was long and pulled back into a ponytail
at the nape of her neck, tied with a leather string, and in her ears were
gold hoops. What I liked was how the extra short hairs around her
face curled. The man, who looked a lot older, had a brown fedora

on his head and wore a darker safari suit. He limped slightly
when he walked.

I was outside alone because my cousins wouldn't let me into the
trap house with them, when she and her husband walked toward the
clubhouse, each carrying a leather gun case. I heard her say to him,
"Think anyone can actually shoot here?"

He shook his head. "Most can't hit the broad side of a barn."

"Good. I plan on winning that gun."

He stopped to open the door for her. "Don't get too set on it. My
trigger finger feels hot today."

She paused, running her eyes up and down him. "Oh, really. Your
trigger wasn't so hot last night," she said.

He stopped, glared at her, and strode ahead, letting the door
close on her.

She stood there a second like she was thinking of turning around,
then took a deep breath and opened the door.

I couldn't keep my eyes off of her. My mom'd left when I was
four and I missed being around someone who smelled nice and wore
lipstick. I got tired of looking at farm wives who wore housedresses
or knit pants that were always too tight. This woman walked with
her head high, like she was somebody special. I wondered what she
thought when she walked into that poor excuse for a clubhouse.

It had been a sheep shed but Billy covered the walls with thin
wood paneling that was supposed to look like knotty pine. On the
north side were three big picture windows, all different sizes, so
you could watch the shoot. The floor was cement. Eight old kitchen
tables—from oak to gray Formica-topped ones—with plenty of old
chairs around each—took up most of the space.

On the west side was a twenty-foot counter, which ran across
the whole front. That's where the food was served by the Women's
Izaak Walton League. Hot Maid Rites, in big homemade buns with
lots of pickles and mustard and wrapped in waxed sheets, sold for
twenty-five cents each. Homemade brownies were a nickel. Little
bags of potato chips cost eight cents. Hershey bars and Salted Nut
Rolls cost ten cents. Along the south wall was a pop machine with

bottles of brilliant orange and red raspberry, root beer and Coca Cola— each twenty-five cents.

If you needed to go to the bathroom, you went outside to the outhouse. There were two of them—one for men and one for women. They were about ten feet apart on the south side, and a short distance away. There was no running water inside the clubhouse. On a card table by the door, Leona, Billy's wife, had two jugs of water if anyone wanted a drink, and a new metal bucket half filled with water, with a bar of Ivory soap floating in it, where the women serving food would dip their hands and dry them on a roller towel hanging from the wall.

My job, and my cousins', was to help search the pasture for good clay pigeons that the trap shooters had missed. We and a few hunting dogs ran out to the pasture between rounds to collect all the good ones. Billy would give us a penny a pigeon, so I could make enough money for a pop and Salted Nut Roll, and on a good day I'd get chips and a Maid Rite, that is if I watched carefully where the pigeons fell. A few of them landed across the pasture fence in a cornfield, and I knew where there was a low spot in the barbed wire section and I'd cross there.

When the woman and man paid their money and got signed up, they sat down and had a cup of coffee out of white glass mugs that said *Billy's Sporting Goods*. She left a red lipstick mark on the rim of the mug. When she was sitting there, she reached into the pocket of her jacket and pulled out a green silk cigarette case. She took out a thin brown cigar, put it to her lips and waited for that man to light it, but he didn't move to do anything. He was sitting with his legs crossed, his one foot dangling, watching out the window. When she touched his arm and motioned for a light, he looked angry. When she saw his look, she got angry, too. She jumped up and walked over to the counter and asked Billy for a book of matches. And Billy, with his greased moustache and slicked-back brown hair, who always had an eye for the ladies, grinned from ear to ear and struck a match. All the while her husband sat there on the chair, not looking, or acting like he wasn't looking. But I saw him peek when Billy's hand trembled as he lit the cigar for her. I noticed how she smiled at Billy and thanked him.

When they both left to go out to shoot, the women talked about them.

"She's the new wife. Well, not so new. Two years they've been married. She's from Canada."

Leona whispered to Gertie Malony. "She's only a year older than his daughter Carol."

And Gertie answered, "But she looks younger. Ain't she pretty though? Much prettier than Mary ever was, God rest her soul. And Mary was such a sour puss. This one's easier to look at in the morning."

Another lady piped up, "Mary may have been ugly but she left him a bundle."

"I hear that this one's a crack shot, wins all sorts of prizes," a woman wrapping Maid Rites said.

"I heard that Carol wouldn't let them stay with her," said Gertie. "They're at the Suburban Motel in town."

"That's half true," Leona added. "Carol said her dad and the new wife—that's what she calls her—won't stay with them because her house ain't fancy enough, which is just fine and dandy with her. She doesn't like to be treated like a servant by someone who's spending all her inheritance money."

"Spending all the money, huh?" asked another woman.

"Yah, they just bought a big house on Lake Huron."

"Then why don't they stay there? Why come back here?" Gertie asked.

"Well, you know, he comes to check out his farms," said Leona.

"Why don't they come in the summer when normal people visit?"

"Carol says she—Aldora, that's her name—has allergies and can't take the humidity and pollen in the air. They wait until after the first hard frost."

Aldora. I said the name over and over. It was a beautiful name. Well, I didn't care what those ladies in their stretchy knit pants thought. I thought she was the prettiest thing I'd ever seen. And I loved how she smoked, blowing that smoke out her mouth like she was getting ready to kiss somebody. When she was halfway done, she'd left the cigar to burn out by itself in the ashtray on the table. Her nails were long and painted maroon, and on her left hand was a fat ruby surrounded by tiny clear stones.

After they went out for their round, I saw a few women step from behind the counter and move to the window to watch. I went outside to be nearer them. I stood next to the snow fence where the spectators had to stand. The five shooters were out in front of the fence at stations about ten feet apart. Each had a station or podium in front of him where he set his shells. Another man, who looked official with a badge on his jacket, was in charge.

He called out, "Round four. Hunters, are you ready?"

And the five trapshooters stood with their shotguns at their shoulders, aiming out at the sky above the bunker. I was so glad I wasn't in the bunker. I would be missing this sight. I watched her, how cool she looked as she stood there, squinting at the sky. Then I saw her lower her gun and the official called, "Wait, the lady's not ready."

And she reached into her top pocket and pulled out a pair of gold-framed glasses—the kind that pilots wear. She was having trouble trying to flip back the bows of the glasses with one hand. The official man moved up to her pretty fast and said, "Let me hold your gun."

There was a titter of giggling as he held the gun while she slipped the sunglasses on. Then she smiled at him, saying "Thank you," and took back the gun.

The official gave the order. "Ready. Commence with shooter number one."

The first guy, in gray work pants and a jacket that had the name *Russ* on it, aimed his gun at the empty sky. He called, "Pull!"

My cousins in the bunker sent a clay pigeon flying off in the direction of the pond at the lower end of the pasture. Russ shot and missed.

When it came to Aldora's turn, she aimed and said, "Pull," but it wasn't loud enough. The official came running down, happy to have a chance to see her again. "Say it louder, Ma'am," he said.

She called out again but still the bunker was quiet.

At that her husband said, "Dammit, just yell it.

Quit being so prissy."

She spun around and aimed her gun right at him. I couldn't see her eyes to tell if she meant it. Everyone watching took a gulp of air and people began to back away from the spectator fence. Her husband just stood there not moving, his gun lowered, and he grinned. Just grinned, nothing more. He didn't move an inch.

The official who was right behind her stepped up quickly and gently pushed the gun around until it faced the empty field. He said something to her in a low voice and then I saw his hand gently pat her on the shoulder.

She lowered the gun for a second, then raised it and called out "Pull!" in a shrill voice that made the official jump. When the pigeon flew straight out over the adjoining cornfield, she followed it and fired. She hit it, sending a spray of clay in the air.

The people behind her clapped and there was one whistle from a high school boy.

It was her husband's turn. He raised his gun and then he did the same thing she'd done. He turned that gun to her and pointed it right at her head and grinned. And it was a grin that made me back away. I saw his yellow teeth in that grin. The official ran over to him and called out, "Sir, lower that gun."

She stood there, her gun at her side, and said, "You don't have the balls to do it."

At that, he pulled the trigger. I screamed. Blood and brains sprayed out as she was thrown backwards. Every person near the fence had blood and gunk splattered on them. Something red hit my forehead and I screamed and wiped it off on the rough wood of the fencing. I looked again. Her nose and one eye were gone. There was a hole that looked like raw hamburger. The other eye was covered in blood and shot peppered her face. She landed on the ground with the back of her head to us. Her blonde hair was covered in blood at the crown. But what got me was that her ponytail at the nape of her neck was perfectly fine. How could that be?

There were screams and sobs and someone was yelling, "Get the doctor!" He was in the clubhouse.

I felt such a sickness take over me that I leaned over and threw up my sandwich and pop. A couple other people were doing the same. A man in khaki pants came running out from the clubhouse. He kneeled over her, blocking us from seeing, but we heard him say, "She's dead."

And before anyone had a chance to take the gun away from her husband, he walked out toward the bunker. The official yelled, "Stop. Put down your weapon," but he didn't stop. He kept on walking toward the bunker and I held my breath. He didn't stop there but just kept going, walking with that limp toward the cornfield. We watched as he broke all the hunting rules of setting your gun down when you crossed a fence. He held the gun in one hand as he crossed and the last we saw he walked right into the field of corn that was ready to be harvested in a week.

A group of men with their guns in hand took off toward the fence. The women were out there crying and calling out, "Leave him alone or you'll get killed."

Then we heard it. A blast coming from the field. And everyone stopped.

For a second or more there was no sound. Then a couple more men took off for the cornfield. Billy and the doctor kneeled next to the woman. Billy covered her with a plastic tablecloth. When the ambulance and sheriff finally got there, I was in the clubhouse. All the mothers made the kids wait inside, and we all watched at the windows, our faces pushed against the glass.

What I remember seeing is the ambulance driving right up to the spectator fence, which was a cheap snow fence, and pushing right through it. Before it stopped, the ambulance man in the passenger side was out the door, running to her. When they got her in the stretcher, I saw her hand with the maroon nails flop out from her body. The ambulance man lifted it and tucked it under the blanket and tied her in.

And that was when I took the cigar. I looked over to the table and saw it in the ashtray, just laying there because she hadn't squished it but had let it burn out. I could see a faint red lipstick mark on the filter end. I took it and put it in my pocket.

I still have that cigar butt. I wrapped it in waxed paper and put it in my shoebox of important things. It's next to the clipping from the newspaper of the murder/suicide. There's a photo of Aldora in her khaki hunting clothes holding a trophy for her marksmanship.

That was the last trapshoot. Billy closed it down and put the sheep back in the pasture. The next October, I was in the truck with my dad driving by the pasture when I saw three sheep going into the clubhouse. The door was gone. And I could barely make out the trap house as it was overgrown with weeds. In another year you wouldn't be able to make out the bunker at all. Nothing would be left to remind us of that day. My cousins said they found the shell casing and the wad that had gone right through his head because it was in the dirt beneath a dried puddle of blood. They didn't tell their dad or mine about it but wrapped the shot in a scrap of denim and hid it in a knothole in their barn. A few times they pulled it out and showed me, but I wouldn't touch that wad. But I touched the thin cigar butt, holding it in my hand like she did and blowing smoke up like I'm kissing the air. And when I do that, I think about her pretty hair like corn silks and how she sticks in my mind. And I think it's a doggoned shame he shot her when she was the one who won all those prizes.

Robert Emmet
Rides
again

1958

I tell this story to show how things
changed between my dad and me after that night. For once we did
something together and that seemed to bring us closer to each other.
Not the kind of closeness that my friend Elizabeth has with her mom
and dad who kiss her morning and night and hug her whenever she
leaves the house. My dad wasn't like that at all. The most he did was
sometimes tap me on the arm when he walked by me at the
kitchen sink.

I stood on a stool that he'd made for me so I could do the dishes
and see out the east window. I like looking toward the river in the
evening because I'd spot my deer heading toward the water for a drink.
I didn't feel so alone when I saw them. They were there almost every
night except during hunting season.

It started when Fergus Mehan, who said he was a descendant
of one of the founding Irish families, got an idea in his head and
wouldn't let it go. Dad said Fergus was only one-fourth Irish and had
no business passing himself off as some patriot. Dad said he probably
never had read one Irish writer in his life. Dad was always reciting

a poem by a man called Yeats (it rhymes with gates), saying, "Romantic Ireland's dead and gone."

The Mehans had only lived on the river road for a few years. Dad said Fergus liked living there rather than in town because there was a barn where he stored new and used washing machines and dryers for his plumbing business. Fergus spent a lot of time in town at meetings organizing an Irish celebration. He wanted to make sure the people of the town remembered the man the town was named after. He was trying to locate the statue of Robert Emmet that had once been in Peter O'Brien's grocery store basement for thirty years after being purchased for three thousand dollars by the Ancient Order of Hibernians who couldn't agree on where to put it. I knew about this because it was in the newspaper all the time.

Now, my Dad was Irish through and through and was related to Robert Emmet. My dad would get mad when he'd read about the statue and throw the paper down. "They never should have let that statue leave town. I told them so." When the people of the town did not donate enough money for a base for the statue to be erected in the town square, Peter O'Brien sold it to someone from Minnesota. Dad had given five dollars and never got his money back. And he was real mad when he found out that Fergus had only donated fifty cents.

One afternoon in June Fergus stopped by to see Dad. Fergus had a green pickup with his name on the door and the slogan—*Keep Your Wife in Hot Water*—running along both sides of the box. Dad and Fergus were talking with their heads bent down. Fergus had a map with him and was pointing to some place on it. I saw Fergus touch my dad on the shoulder, but my dad shook his head and took off his cap. This went on for a few minutes and then Fergus left.

That night Dad was restless. When I asked him what was wrong, he said, "Nothing."

But I knew better. He kept studying the map of Minnesota and adding up miles. "Why didn't you go with Fergus?"

"I'm not a thief," he said and hit the table with his fist.

"What's he stealing?"

"Nothing. Just go to bed."

I looked at the clock. It was a quarter to nine. "What time is he leaving?"

"Nine."

"You can still go," I said.

"Naw, can't leave you alone all night."

"Dad, I'm eight years old. I can take care of myself." But I was hoping he wouldn't leave me.

"No. I'm not going."

I went to bed that June evening with the windows wide open and a breeze coming in. I wouldn't need a fan. It was cool, just the way I liked it. Some of spring, not quite worn off, was still in the air and that was the best way to sleep. I pulled up my sheet and quilt. It was my favorite quilt. It had been my mom's when she married Dad. I liked to look at the different squares of material and imagine what dresses or blouses she'd worn. Dad said her grandmother had helped her make it. My mom never had a mom either. Her mom had died when she was six years old so she was raised by her grandma. Sometimes I wonder what went wrong. Why did she leave? Dad just said she wasn't cut out for farming and he never should have brought her here. It was too dull for her. She liked to be around lots of people. Before they were married she'd worked in the Shamrock Tavern as a waitress and bartender. After they were married she worked a few weekends a month. Dad never talks about her and has hidden all her pictures. I've searched in his room, or what used to be their room, and I can't find anything but a picture of a pretty garden with a bench that Mom hung above their bed.

About nine o'clock the next morning, Fergus drove in the yard. He was acting all riled up— gesturing, laughing, and talking loudly. When he left, my dad came in the house and said we were going to Emmetsburg.

All the way in Dad was quiet. "What are we going to see?" I asked.

"Just want to see if Fergus's leading me on."

We drove past Fergus's place on the river road. His truck was gone. Dad slowed down when we got to Ted's grocery.

"What are you looking for?"

"Nothing," he said again. Why did he always say nothing when he knew it wasn't nothing?

At the main intersection we saw a group of men milling around. And there it was. A statue of a man, about ten feet high, right in front of the bank. The statue had a green felt derby on its head.

"Damn. He wasn't pulling my leg," Dad said.

"Who is it?" I asked, but I sort of knew.

"Robert Emmet."

"Did Fergus do this? Is this what he wanted you to do?"

"Now you keep quiet about this."

The men touched and stroked the statue like they were trying to be sure it was real. A man with a camera was taking pictures and a policeman was taking notes on a pad of paper.

On Thursday the newspaper carried a picture of the statue on the front page. It told the story of a group of men going to Deep Haven, Minnesota, and stealing it. The owners were not too happy and were filing charges. The reporter said they didn't know the names of the bandits but police were investigating. I felt pretty good since I could tell them the name of one and then I was so glad my dad hadn't done this. What if they all would get arrested? What if my dad would go to jail for a long time and I'd be left alone?

The next afternoon Fergus Mehan stopped again. I made sure I stayed hidden in the machine shed. Fergus said, "They say a group of them are coming down from Minnesota and they're going to do to the statue what was done to Robert in real life."

My dad said, "You mean, hang him?"

Fergus chuckled. "Might not have a rope strong enough. No, they plan on taking his head off."

"Well now, how are they going to do that to a bronze statue?"

Fergus looked around like someone might be listening. "A hacksaw, that's how."

"Yup, that would do it."

"So we're posting a guard tonight and tomorrow. Want to come and help us watch?"

"I can't leave Brigid alone."

Fergus kicked the dirt. "Yah, I forgot about the girl. I guess you can't go. Well, I'll let you know what happens."

After Fergus left, I stepped out and told my dad, "You can go. I'll be okay."

"Nope. Can't."

"What if you just go for a few hours? Don't stay there the whole night."

Dad thought about that awhile but it didn't satisfy him.

"What if I go with you and sleep in the truck?"

"But will you sleep?"

"Sure will. I'll take my pillow and quilt. You lock the door and I'll be fine."

At that idea Dad seemed to perk up. "Just for a few hours, okay? And I'll check on you every half hour."

I felt excited. He was going to do it. I was dying to see what was happening. And I knew that I'd never sleep.

A half hour later we were headed to town and I was hugging my pillow. I felt like a conspirator with Dad. When we got to the main street intersection, the statue was gone. Dad said they moved him to the courthouse square, a block away. We saw a bunch of men surrounding the statue. Some of the men had brought lawn chairs. Dad had forgotten his chair, but he had a couple bales of hay in the back. He and a few men grabbed them and sat on them. Dad parked on the north side of the square and I left the window open. Dad told me I had to stay inside, but if I had to go to the bathroom he'd take me to the tavern across the street.

After two hours of waiting and listening to the muffled conversations of men who were taking turns going into the tavern and coming out a little happier and funnier, I saw two car loads of men drive by. The cars had Minnesota plates. One group was in an old Cadillac and another was in a Buick. They drove around and around the square until Fergus yelled out, "Are you too chicken to get out?"

And one of the men in the second car yelled back, "Why don't you come after us, you mackerel-snapping thieves!"

That did it. The men jumped in their cars and my dad came

running to our truck and we all took off after them. The Minnesota cars drove out of town heading toward the town of Mallard. They were going pretty darn fast. My dad was smiling and I smelled beer on him. I counted four cars and our pickup and another pickup in the procession. We went all the way to Mallard, past the Duck In sandwich shop, when they turned right and headed down the main street. Pretty soon we were all following each other. When we pulled to a stop at the gas station, all the men got out and waved their hands and talked loudly. I heard one say, "They must know someone here. Bet your sweet ass they drove into someone's garage. Dammit to hell."

"Let's split up. Three go to the south and circle back to Main and three go to the north. Meet back here in fifteen minutes."

So that's what we did. Dad and I were part of the south team but we didn't see the Cad or the Buick. It sure was fun driving with our lights off like we were detectives hot on a case. I'd never seen Dad so excited. A half hour later we headed back to Emmetsburg and when we got there we saw two police cars in front of the statue of Robert Emmet.

He was headless.

"God damn," Dad swore. "We were tricked."

For some reason that bothered Dad more than anything. Robert Emmet had lost his head and Dad was determined to put it back on. He could use a torch and braze it. But the police said he would have to wait. The head was evidence. They were going to find the culprits.

Dad didn't like being tricked. He came home that night and sat in his rocker and drank from his bottle of whiskey that he kept in his gun cabinet in the basement. I don't know how long he sat there rocking back and forth but the next morning he was still in bed when I got up at nine o'clock. It was a good thing he didn't have a baling job lined up.

I smelled his sickness before I even got to his room. Dad was sleeping but I saw he had a bucket near his bed. I about got sick when I looked inside. Dad stayed in bed until noon. I made him some tea but he hardly touched it. He needed some ginger ale or 7-Up but we didn't have any. He said he'd drive to Osgood, a poor excuse of a town only a mile away in the river bottomland. The town had four houses, a grain elevator, lots of gravel pits and a grocery store. Dad drove slowly but when we went over the wooden bridge over the west branch of the Des Moines, the pickup shook and Dad moaned. His face was pale.

It took five minutes to get there. Dad said I had to run inside and look for the pop. The wooden screen door banged when I entered. Arnold Carney looked up from behind the counter where he was reading the *Emmetsburg Democrat*. I waved and kept moving. The store had two aisles. Dad got rice once and we had to throw the bag away because it was full of maggots. The only things that were fresh were the loaves of Wonder Bread and Twinkies, which the bread man dropped off weekly. Every time I went by the Breck shampoo I always saw the same six bottles of nail polish. Mom'd left a bottle just like that in the medicine cabinet.

The pop and beer in the back of the store were stacked on top of the butcher counter. They hadn't sold meat, except hot dogs, bacon, and bologna, for a long time. I saw bottles of Coke and cans of Hamms and Grain Belt. Near the orange pop was the 7-Up. I grabbed a six-pack of green bottles and walked toward the counter. A box of Twin Bing candy bars was right beside the register. I wanted one but Dad hadn't given me enough money. I got the pop. And when I brought it to the pickup Dad was waiting with a pop opener that he always kept on his key ring. He opened a bottle and took a long drink. He seemed to perk up.

"Why does pop make you better?"

"I don't know. Might be the bubbles in it. They seem to do something to the acid in my stomach."

"Do you want one?" Dad asked, looking at me while he took another drink.

I nodded and he opened a bottle for me. It seemed to have more bubbles. It was warm.

We drove home, each holding our pop. Dad put his between his legs to hold it still. I held mine.

"Do you think you can put that head back on Robert Emmet?" I asked.

Dad had the window open and his arm rested there. It was windy and hot. "With a torch I might be able to do it."

"But it won't look the same," I added.

"I suppose it won't be like it was."

"Dad, why are you so mad about this? Are we related to that man?"

"Yup, but that's not the reason. I just don't like to be tricked. It burns me."

I figured now was as good a time as any to ask. "Did Mom trick you?"

Dad stiffened and he didn't even turn toward me. He just stared ahead. Had he heard?

I asked again. This time he said, "What the hell are you talking about?"

"You know, when she left home." I held the pop so tight my fingers hurt.

"Well, I suppose. She took all the money we had saved. I guess you could call that tricking me."

And she tricked me, too. I remember waking up one morning and Mom was gone. "Why did she do it?"

Dad's face tightened. "You're too young to understand."

"I'm not. I'm going to be in fourth grade."

"God, that's young."

"Someone at school said she ran off to Las Vegas."

Dad slammed on the brakes of the truck and opened the door. I grabbed the bottle of pop between his legs. The truck was still moving but Dad was leaning over throwing up. All that good pop was ending up on the ground.

Dad pulled himself back up and moaned. Then he reached for his pop bottle, took a swig and swished the stuff in his mouth and spit it out. He wiped his mouth with his hand.

"You okay?"

"Nope. I feel like sh—." He never finished.

I was silent while he crossed the bridge again and he seemed to be breathing deeply.

We pulled up to the house and Dad turned off the pickup.

He looked at me with his pale face and said, "She's gone and we're doing just fine without her. Aren't we?"

How did I tell him that we weren't doing just fine? I wanted a mom. I wanted someone who could make the living room look nice. It was a mess with piles of newspapers and coffee cups and cereal bowls on the end table. The walls were bare. Dad'd taken down the pictures—and I felt like we were always getting ready to move. And Dad still had my dollhouse in the corner. I played with it sometimes but I didn't want people to know that. But then no one came inside the house. Now I'd be embarrassed to have anyone spend the night. Besides, once I phoned Elizabeth who lived in town and I'd asked her to sleep over. Her mom had said no. I knew it was because of Mom leaving and Dad being alone with me.

Dad went to bed and I wondered what to do. I had a few books from the library that I hadn't finished yet. Dad took me to the library every two weeks on Saturday. I usually got a grocery bag full of books and Dad picked out a few westerns and lots of travel books. When I asked why he always got those books about strange places he said, "Well, maybe when you're grown up I'll go to Greece. Always wanted to see those statues with missing parts." Then he'd show me some lady without arms and a head.

And then it hit me right there. Missing parts. My, oh my. Robert Emmet had a big missing part.

Dad slept all afternoon and got up about six. He sat at the table, leaning his chin on his hands and looking pretty peaked. I fixed him a bologna sandwich with pickles and horseradish.

"Dad, you know what. It might not be so bad about Robert Emmet. Now he's just like those Greek statues."

"What?"

"Those statues in those books from the library."

"Oh."

"Well, they don't have heads either," I said.

"Those are ancient. It's okay if their heads are gone." Dad held the sandwich in his hand and looked at it, then put it down.

"Aren't you going to eat that?"

"You can have it."

I moved the plate in front of me and downed the sandwich in five bites. It was good. I make a mean sandwich when I set my mind to it. Tomorrow I'd try to make meatloaf like Mom used to make. Dad always liked that. And while I waited for the meatloaf to bake, I'd take out that book on Greece and try to find a statue that was headless just like Robert Emmet was. If I showed it to Dad, he might feel better and eat a good meal for a change.

the Woman who was part man

1959

I live with my dad on the river road. He's had me ever since Mom left when I was four. He runs a baler in summer and a combine in fall and does plowing for farmers in the spring. We make our money from doing other people's once-a-year work. Dad says he gets fed well because balers and harvesters get served the best food, although lately he's been complaining that the farm women who work in town now are shirking their duty. Some of the men take the balers to Pearl's or the Redwood Cafe but it isn't the same. Dad misses the pie and rhubarb crisp.

Lately he's been looking at me real strange when I come into the kitchen in my underpants after taking a bath. The other day he told me to put on a tee shirt and to start wearing one from now on. I knew what he was trying to tell me. I was starting to grow on top. They ache a little and seem pointier, especially when I wear a cotton shirt. This next year in sixth grade we're supposed to get "the talk" and I'm getting pretty nervous about it, since a parent's supposed to come to one of the sessions. The nurse tells parents, mostly moms, how to talk to their kids about this sex stuff and she says she can get even the shyest person to open up about it. But she hasn't met my dad.

He can't even talk when I ask him about Adelaide, the woman who is part man. When I say that, he harrumphs and says, "She's not part man. She just looks like one."

We have this same conversation every June right after she comes to line him up to bale hay. When you first see her driving into the lane in her red International truck, you think it's a man. There's not much on the surface to separate her from farmers. But Dad says she isn't exactly a farmer or a man for that matter. She has a few horses and a field of alfalfa, which she has my dad bale for her every summer. Adelaide was married once to a real old guy who died shortly after the wedding. Talk said she helped him along a bit. He left her the buildings and thirty acres. Dad said it was all right and legal because there'd been a will. Adelaide left the county for a few years right afterwards and when she came back she stayed to herself.

This June when she drove in the lane in her truck, she had someone else in the cab with her. Adelaide was easy to spot because she wore a cowboy hat, jeans, and a plaid shirt with a vest. For as long as I've known Adelaide she's worn that same leather vest. And in the pocket she kept her Lucky Strikes and matches. She cut her hair short, parted it on the side, and combed it behind her ears. About three times a year she'd have the barber trim it real close so she didn't have to do much with it. Just waited for it to grow. Dad said she saved money having a barber do it. "At a beauty parlor they rob you blind," he said. As soon as I asked, "Did Mom go there?" he turned away.

He said, "Once. Yup, got one of those perms." I held onto that information like it was gold, and I imagined her head surrounded by soft blonde curls that smelled like honeysuckle.

Adelaide got out of the truck and walked over to my dad who was working on our Farmall H again. She walked right up to that tractor and studied it, then when my dad saw her standing there with her fingers tucked into the front pocket of her jeans, he put his wrench in his left hand and stepped around to shake her hand. She pulled her right hand out and squared her shoulders and stepped forward.

She was the only woman I knew of who could shake hands like a man and do it right.

I was standing near the open door of the machine shed putting air in my bike tire when I looked up and heard her say, "It's ready."

Dad nodded. "How about tomorrow? Let's say about ten."

"Same price?" she asked.

Dad nodded.

And she tipped her hat and walked away. That was that.

When she opened the door to her truck, a strange-looking girl jumped out and began running toward the swing set. Adelaide didn't run but walked with long steps toward this girl in overalls with curly red hair. Her head was big, her skin pale; she looked chubby, almost doughy. And she ran like she had one leg shorter than the other. She appeared to be about my age, maybe older, but she acted like she was four years old. She ran straight for the see-saw that Dad had built at one end of the swing set. She sat down, sort of, and lifted her butt off, jumping up and down, motioning for Adelaide to hurry up. I'd have thought that Adelaide would have told her to get back to the truck, but she went to the other end and sat down and then kicked up with her booted feet. They went up and down on the see-saw and seemed to be in no hurry to leave. Adelaide was careful not to push off too strongly and she let the girl go only so high.

Just then I stepped out from the machine shed and moved toward my dad who was also watching them.

"Hey, they didn't even ask." I motioned to the see-saw.

Dad pushed back his straw hat with the wrench and said, "They're not hurting anything."

"That kid sure looks stupid to me," I said.

"Doesn't have both oars in the water."

"What do you mean?"

"Terry's feeble-minded. Born that way," he answered.

"How come I haven't seen her?"

"Adelaide keeps her at a special school, but I heard she can't afford it anymore. So she brought her home."

I watched as this girl made ooh and aah noises while she went up and down. She drooled like she'd just eaten some horseradish root.

"Gosh, I hope she doesn't get that spit all over things," I moaned.

"Spit won't hurt anything," Dad said, then turned and went back to his fixing.

I walked toward the see-saw, wishing I could be invisible so I could watch them. As I got nearer, Adelaide stopped and motioned for the girl to follow her to the truck. But the girl had seen me and came racing up to me like she was going to throw her arms around me. When I saw that slobber on her face and snot running from her nose, I turned and ran like the wind.

A wail came from her as I rounded the machine shed, so I stopped and peered around the corner. But she wasn't crying, she was standing there giggling and looking around like she'd seen fireworks. Then Adelaide came forward and led her back to the truck.

The next day I went along, riding on the back of the flatbed. It would take us one afternoon to do Adelaide's small field. She used the hay for her horses that she kept in her barn.

When we drove into Adelaide's field lane across from her house and barn and tumble-down sheds, I spotted the girl sitting on the white propane tank. She was riding the tank, kicking it, like it was a surly horse. I was surprised that her mom let her do this. Dad wouldn't let me do it because he said the tank could blow up. While Dad was busy getting the baler ready, I walked across the road and got nearer to the tank and stood there watching her. When she saw me coming, she stopped kicking the tank and just watched me. Her eyes were blue with lots of red lines running through. She had those same dark blue overalls on. Her white tee shirt was tight underneath, and I saw breasts or maybe they were mounds of fat. Under her chin was another glob of fat. I kept studying her and trying to figure out if she was my age or older. That went on for about five minutes until I couldn't stand it anymore. I kicked at the gravel beneath my feet and leaned over and picked up a black rock, which I threw at a tree. Then I saw that she had slipped off the tank and was motioning for me to follow her.

She led me to the back of the house where the grass was high and there were all sorts of old boxes and pieces of junk—metal tractor seats, mufflers, a broken toilet bowl, a tricycle with one wheel, oil drums, tractor and car tires, a sleigh missing a runner, and a saddle on another barrel. I decided right then this kid loved to pretend she was riding a horse. But she didn't get on that barrel. Instead she climbed a mulberry tree and began picking the dark berries and eating them.

She picked a few more and held out her hand to me. She had squeezed too hard and they were squished. I felt my stomach leap and jump when I saw the purple slobber on her chin. So I took off running around the house and heading back to the safety of the flatbed. When I got there, Dad and Adelaide were ready to go to the field.

That's when Dad said, "You wait here."

"But I want to ride in the wagon."

"Nope, not today." Last year I'd ridden there and had tried to help Adelaide stack the bales.

"What am I supposed to do?"

"Play with Terry."

I looked at Dad and huffed. "No way. I'm walking home."

Dad looked at me and said, "I told Adelaide you'd watch Terry."

I rolled my eyes but I didn't say anything because Dad was giving me one of his mean looks. So I turned back and saw that this dimwit was leading a spotted pony toward me. A Shetland pony who was no bigger than she was. When she got nearer, she handed me the reins. I held them while she threw herself over the pony, and then she motioned for me to give the reins back. I did. With a yelp of glee, she kicked the pony and took off trotting down the lane toward the open road. I watched them jump up and down, up and down, the jerking motion shaking her curls and her tummy.

She turned the pony around and came back to me. She slid off and motioned for me to get on. I shook my head but she persisted. So I got on, feeling the heat of the pony's body on my bare legs. The pony felt damp and I wished I had long pants on. I was almost lying on the pony, my arms around its neck, my face in the mane. And this girl saw that I was afraid and began leading the pony down the lane, walking fast. The pony kept nudging her back and she giggled.

At the end of the lane she turned me around and put the reins over the pony's head and handed them to me.

"What do I do? How do I stop it?"

She motioned for me to pull back and said, "Whoa, whoa."

"But I don't know its name. What's its name," I said, talking carefully so she could figure it out.

She giggled and pointed to the leather strap that went behind its ears. The word Peanut was cut into the leather. I said, "Peanut," and she shook her head up and down.

Then she gave Peanut a pat on his butt and we were off trotting. My body was jolted and my legs felt like they were going to split apart. I wondered if this was going to do anything to my privates. They felt stretched and sore and hot.

While Peanut trotted, Terry ran behind me making oohing and laughing noises. Her arms were waving and clapping. I pulled back on the reins and Peanut didn't like it. He shook his head so his mane tossed and I pulled again, this time hard. He stopped and snorted and tried to nip at my knee.

I slid off and stepped back. Terry grabbed the bridle and rubbed Peanut's nose.

"You . . . li-i-ike?" she asked. The words sounded thick, like her tongue was too big for her mouth.

God, she was weird and I was too chicken to tell her that I hated it, so instead I just smiled. It hadn't been as bad as I thought, but I was glad I was standing on the ground.

She led the pony back to the paddock, opened the gate, and led him in and then slipped off his bridle. She made cooing noises as she did this and rubbed his nose. The pony stepped forward and paused, stretching its legs out. Water splashed, and I saw a stream of yellow pee coming from underneath. I leaned over and looked. It was a long thing. It scared me how red it was and how big it was.

Then Terry unzipped her overalls and pulled out a long thing, too, and pissed right there, standing with her or his legs apart like the pony was doing.

My eyes were bulging and my mouth was dry as I watched this
stream arch out from that pink thing. I wondered if her Mom pissed
like that or did she squat like I had to. Nothing made sense anymore.
Then I took off running for home, not even caring if I left that weird
kid outside. I just wanted to be alone to think.

Once I made it to my house, I ran inside and upstairs to my
bedroom. In my top drawer I kept a couple snapshots of my mother.
The one I liked the best was when she was holding me in her lap when
I was a baby about eight months old. She had on a yellow dress that
was soft and loose. She was smiling at me like she was making some
baby cooing sounds and I was giggling. We both looked happy. And
when I studied this picture I wondered why she left. How could she
leave such a cute little thing? Did I do something to make her mad?
Did my dad make her mad? Maybe he wasn't nice enough to her.
Maybe he didn't buy her flowers or chocolates like other husbands
did on TV shows. But there was no doubt that Mom was a woman.
I could see the bulge of her breasts through the yellow fabric. They
weren't really big but just a nice size. And the yellow color of the dress
showed that Mom was tan all over. She looked healthy and alive—not
pasty white like that kid or boy or whatever it was.

And I wondered what Dad had done with Mom's clothes. They
disappeared one night. For months and months, I'd gone to Mom's
dresser drawers and had felt the soft tee shirts and silky pajamas.
Mom hadn't taken much when she'd left. In the bedroom closet
that my parents had shared were a few dresses on hangers. And
I remembered seeing the yellow dress. I'd go in that closet, close
the door and sit right underneath that dress and take in Mom's smell.
Mom wore some oil on her skin that smelled like incense and that
smell hung in the closet for a long time, that is until the day I opened
the closet and the dresses were all gone. I cried and asked Dad what
had happened to them. He said he'd given them to the church women
who were always collecting clothes for the poor. And I hated him
then for doing that. Those were my dresses, too. They were all I had
left of Mom.

Right after the dresses disappeared I'd gone through every drawer in their bedroom and had found these snapshots. I hadn't told Dad about them. I just kept them. I also found a tube of lipstick and some nail polish and a hairbrush and an earring that didn't have a mate. It was gold with beads and it looked like something an Indian woman would wear. And I put these things in my shoebox of stuff.

A few hours later Dad drove in the lane with the baler. He came into the house and yelled at me. I was upstairs in my room with my shoebox of stuff spread out on the bed.

He stood at my door and said, "Where did you go? I told you to watch Adelaide's girl."

"Girl, huh? She isn't any girl, Dad."

Dad's face was dirty and his eyes were red from all the dust. He must have rubbed them. "What are you talking about?"

And I told him what I saw and he seemed surprised, too. Real surprised. And I said that maybe Adelaide was a boy, too. And Dad said, no. She had a baby. Men don't have babies. Then he walked over to my pictures of Mom and picked up the one with her in the yellow dress.

"And I'm not going to the barber anymore to get my hair cut. I'm growing it out and I'm going to have curls like Mom," I said.

My hair was cut straight all the way around my head, since Dad said it was easier to take care of. He took me to the barber when he went every couple of months. And I got this stupid cut that made me look like the little Dutch Boy on the can of paint. "And I want to wear something besides jeans."

My dad was real quiet. He just held that photo in his hand and looked at it for a long time. "You shouldn't have left that . . . boy alone. Adelaide was upset."

"Well, so was I."

Later on that night I saw Dad go into the garage with a ladder and I figured he was going up into the attic. When I was almost asleep, he came into my room and placed something on the bottom of my bed. After he left I got up and looked. It was the yellow dress. I gathered it to me and put my face into the fabric, breathing as deeply as I could.

The smell was still there. Incense. Mom.

The dress wasn't as bright yellow as it was in the photo but it was mine now. I hung it behind my door so I could look at it every day. And when Dad left to go check on a baling job the next morning, I climbed up the ladder to the attic. I found all the clothes and more pictures of me and Mom and Dad. One I really liked was all three of us together at my birthday. There were two candles in a white cake. Mom had on an African-fabric dress with long earrings dropping to her shoulders. Her hair was pulled back and I could see the shape of her face—an oval.

Some time later, I heard someone climbing the ladder. It was Dad. "You shouldn't be up here. It's too hot and you could pass out."

I didn't even listen to him. "I want these things for me." And he helped me take the boxes down and I spent the day sorting through the stuff.

That July I didn't go to the barber, and when it came time for buying school clothes I said I wanted a dress, and I didn't want one from Farm and Home Supply. I wanted a nice one. And I made my dad go into Mary's Style Shop and I tried on four dresses. Dad got me one of them and two pairs of trousers that were made of soft fabric. The lady said I needed to get tops to match. And I loved the tops that weren't like boys'. They had fancy buttons and one had a hand-crocheted daisy on the collar.

I know I don't want to look like Adelaide with her man's haircut that's supposed to be easy to take care of. At night after I wash my hair, I use Mom's brush and try to pull it down and stretch it to make it longer. Soon it will touch my jaw and then maybe I can get one of those perms so it will curl softly like Mom's did in the picture.

the Cockfight

1960

One morning in May when the oak and ash trees had opened up, we saw a sight that made even the bus driver stop and stare. High on a branch of an oak tree hung one of the brown-feathered roosters. A clothesline rope was around its neck and the rope was tangled in a branch. The rooster's neck was stretched like the neck of a water balloon. Its body looked heavy and full, like it was ready to explode. It was so high up that no one could get it down. The Daley boys certainly wouldn't climb the tree to get it. And I heard from one of the kids on the bus that Mr. Daley tried to shoot at the rope with his .22 but he missed and eventually ran out of shells.

Day after day we watched that rooster spoil and rot before our eyes. Then one morning it was just a carcass of guts suspended there. Crows were flying around it, picking at a gizzard or some organ hanging by a dried sinew. The head and neck were still in the noose.

I said to Elmer, the oldest Daley boy, who was a sophomore, "How'd it happen? How'd it get up there?"

Elmer looked up from his book and said, "Mom did it."

And his younger brother Eustace, a freshman, added, "Dad took her babysitting money."

The next day we saw a hand-painted sign nailed to the fence post near the garden—*ROOSTERS FOR SALE*. That was when I got myself involved in the Daley family.

The school bus stopped in front of their house twice a day. Most farmhouses sat back a ways, having long lanes and lots of grass in the front yard. But this house rented by the Daleys sat right next to the narrow ditch alongside the gravel river road. It was a small house—dirty-white with a floppy front screen door that opened up to four cracked cement steps and a small lilac bush at the bottom.

Mrs. Daley babysat for a few mothers who worked in town. From what I could see from the bus, which sat up high enough for me to look inside their house, the place wasn't too clean. I saw something smeared on the front picture window, a riding horse and a pedal-car parked in front of the TV, and baskets of clothes near a gold couch that had a worn arm with white stuff poking out. Many afternoons on my way home on the bus I saw Mrs. Daley sitting in a wood rocker folding towels that came off the clothesline behind the house. The TV was tuned to *Heckle and Jeckle* and I could watch it. It was strange watching TV from behind two layers of glass. There must have been six or seven children in that living room. And many times I saw them lined up on the couch sucking their thumbs as they stared at Daffy Duck.

Mr. Daley wasn't a farmer. He made his money mowing church lawns in town. In winter he did snow removal. He put a blade on his truck and headed to town, forgetting to do his own lane.

The Daleys were too poor to own this acreage with a chicken house, a long skinny shed, and a rickety garage. There was a big garden to the north of the place. The land around the acreage was farmed by J.B. Bruning, who seemed to own most of the section. Mrs. Daley had J.B. plow up her garden plot each spring so she could plant green beans, tomatoes, potatoes, and squash. Most folks knew that she kept the family alive with her babysitting money, her eggs,

and garden produce. Every August at the county fair, she won
a couple blue ribbons for her giant squash.

The only things Mr. Daley had to be proud of were his prized
roosters, which he trained to strut around the yard and fly at anyone
who got out of a car. You didn't hear them until you felt their beaks
pecking at you and their wings flapping as they flew at your head.
The Fuller Brush man claimed he was so startled that he fell down,
and before he could get up the roosters had attacked his face,
pecking him and taking flesh. He was suing Daleys, but everyone
laughed because they knew he wouldn't get anything from a family
that had nothing.

Mr. Daley kept the roosters in the long skinny shed, and
he'd rigged up individual wire pens for each one. It looked like
a dog kennel but not a nice dog kennel. He'd taken a saw and cut
out doorways—six of them big enough so he could crawl through
to go into their wire pens to feed and water them. Inside he'd put up
plywood dividers. Fighting roosters had to be separated. But twice
a day he let his roosters out for a walk, usually only one or two at
a time. When mothers dropped off their children, they all looked
around before opening their car doors, and then they ran toward
the back steps.

The story was that Mrs. Daley kept her babysitting money in
a Mason jar hidden behind her sugar and flour canisters. She carefully
doled out the money to her two sons when they needed new jeans or
eyeglasses. They were smart boys—always reading something—and
that's why their eyes were so bad. Whenever the bus would stop to
pick them up, they'd be sitting at the kitchen table reading. They'd
come out to the bus, reading as they walked, and the bus driver
would honk and say, "Boys, move it or, darnit, I'm leaving you." But
he never left them.

The books they read were from the public library and everyone
knew when they'd gotten a book that the Daley boys had read
because it was dog-eared and smeared with peanut butter and drops
of rhubarb jelly. The boys could eat and read at the same time. They
were big boys and big readers.

At school lunch, which they got free, they ate and ate. If you didn't like something, then you scooped it onto their plates and they just nodded and kept on eating. The principal had a rule that they couldn't bring books into the lunchroom but the Daley boys brought in newspapers, which they grabbed from the janitor's closet. And they usually found some crossword puzzle that they worked on together. They didn't have friends except Jeremiah Lammers, who would read anything and everything about horses. He would sit next to them and draw horse heads on the napkins. He didn't eat like the Daley boys; he was skinny and runty. He was going to be a jockey and ride in the Kentucky Derby someday.

That Tuesday afternoon after I got off the bus, I rode my bike down to the Daley place, which was about three-fourths of a mile from my farm. There was something about those roosters that fascinated me. Three of them were fancy brown and red ones and they just looked mean. There were three regular white ones but somehow their training made them show-offy, too.

When I got into the yard, which was full of chicken droppings, I saw that the six roosters were in their pens. As I walked toward them, one flew at me but hit the wire and dropped back down.

Mrs. Daley came out to the back step and called out, "What'ya doing?"

"Looking at your roosters. How much you asking?"

She cocked her head and studied me. Then she started down the three back steps and limped over to me. Her legs were all swollen, especially the ankles, and she seemed to struggle with every step.

"Now why would a young girl like you want these roosters?" she asked as she got nearer.

"They're sort of pretty."

"Pretty?" she huffed. "They're mean, not pretty."

She stood beside me, so close that I smelled her sweat and sweet bacon-like odor.

"What are you asking?" I said, inching away from her.

"Honey, I don't think you want them. They've been trained to attack anyone who gets near them."

"How much?"

She paused and reached into the sleeve of her faded housedress and pulled out a red bandana. She used only one hand to hold the cloth, and she took a deep breath and blew. I looked away because I didn't want to see anything dripping out from the cloth. She wiped her nose with one hand and put it back into her sleeve.

That's when I saw that one arm wasn't quite the same size as the other. It was shorter and bony and hung there. "Can you use that?" I asked, motioning to her arm.

"A little. I got it cut bad when I was a girl and it never has worked right. But I know how to make it do what I need it to." And she lifted it to her glasses and took them off and put them back on to show me that she could make it work. But it looked like she was trying hard.

"How do you change diapers?"

"I change them just fine."

The back door slammed and I saw Elmer at the step holding a book. "Ma, the baby's crying."

"Pick her up," she called.

Elmer went back in and a few minutes later he was back outside on the step, holding a baby on his shoulder, patting it gently and sort of rocking back and forth. He didn't have a book in his hand.

"What does she want?" he yelled, acting like I wasn't standing there.

"She wants to buy some roosters."

"Why?" he asked, stepping carefully down the stairs.

I didn't know what to answer. "Just because I want to," I said.

He squinted at me and wrinkled his nose.

"I won't sell them to her," his mom said to him. And then she turned to me. "A young girl shouldn't be having fighting roosters."

"But what if I have money?"

Mrs. Daley laughed. "How much do you have?"

"Five dollars and twenty-eight cents."

"That's not enough," said Elmer. "They're real special birds, you know. They've been trained."

My face was getting hotter. "How much do they cost?"

Elmer looked at his mom and then he handed her the baby. They both seemed to be figuring things out in their heads.

Mrs. Daley harrumphed with her throat and said, "Even if you had the money, I wouldn't sell you one. They'd peck your eyes out and I'm sure your daddy wouldn't be too happy to have his girl blinded by a mean rooster."

Elmer walked over to the pen and stood there silent a second and then he jumped at the pen, making a mean face and waving his arms. The roosters scrunched up their necks and flew at him but they hit the fence. Elmer laughed and charged at them again.

"Cut it out," Mrs. Daley warned. "We don't want them all riled."

"Why do you want them to be so mean?" I asked.

Elmer looked at me through his thick glasses and grinned. "You are a stupid girl, aren't you?"

I was stung by his words and stepped back.

Mrs. Daley growled at him. "Stop acting like your old man. She just asked a question and you don't have to be so ornery." She turned toward me and said, "Sorry, Honey. The dark-colored ones are fighting cocks. They're raised to kill other roosters."

"How do they kill?"

Elmer laughed. "We put gaffs on their spurs. They attack with their feet and tear each other apart in no time."

"Gaffs?"

"They're like barbs on a fence. They cut like the devil," Elmer said.

Mrs. Daley nodded. "They sometimes peck each other to death."

"But how come they aren't pecking each other now?" I asked.

"Oh, they do," said Mrs. Daley rocking back and forth on her feet trying to lull the baby. "Just last week two walls in the shed fell down and we had to pull them roosters apart or we'd have lost one or two."

"Last month they got one of the weaker white ones," said Elmer. "Once a bird shows that it's weak they all gang up and peck it until it's dead."

"You'd better skedaddle on home, Brigid. Your daddy's probably wondering where you are."

"Is that why that bird was up in the tree? Was that the one that got pecked to death?"

Elmer started snickering. "Naw, there wasn't enough left of the pecked bird to throw."

"Well, how'd that one get up in the tree?"

Mrs. Daley gave her son a look and then she turned toward me. "Now don't be so nosy. We're not selling you the bird or answering any more questions. I got to get this baby in the house."

She turned and headed toward the back door where a little three-year-old was leaning against the screen, holding a piece of bread.

A few days later, on Saturday, I was on my bike on the river road after taking my dad a late snack. He was helping J.B. Bruning plant soybeans. Dad always found work helping farmers who got behind in their planting. I was pushing my bike up the hill toward the Fogarty place, which J.B. owned and farmed—he just rented the buildings and a few acres for hay to the Fogartys—when I spotted Mr. Daley's '55 Dodge truck with his make-shift cages in the back, partially covered, heading down the field lane that led back to the river in the bottomlands. It was the lane used by hunters because J.B. had built a tree house for a deer blind and had fixed up an old barn for hunters to warm themselves. Every year in November and December that field lane got lots of use. I turned my bike around and followed the trail until I came to the barn. Trucks and cars were already there. I hid my bike in the trees and crept up to the shed. Someone had put a new door on it. My dad told me never to go back by the shed in spring and summer because they had cockfights there. They were illegal and a bad element went to them.

I looked through the cracks in the wall. Men were standing around a circle of double-high chicken wire. Mr. Daley was holding his rooster, talking to it. Across from him in the ring was another man, holding his bird and stroking its back. Each man was behind a white line drawn on the dirt floor. The lines were about eight to ten feet apart.

The birds were straining to break free—they were trembling and puffing themselves up. Mr. Daley held the bird under his arm, took a hunk of cotton and dipped it in a bucket of water and dribbled a few drops in his rooster's mouth. Then he put water on the silver two-inch gaffs. With a nod from the man in the center of the ring, Mr. Daley and the other man held their roosters down on the white line. When the referee called out, "Pit 'em," both let go and the birds launched themselves at each other. Men hooted and whistled. There was a flurry of feathers and flapping and tumbling and a clinking of gaffs and dirt flying. Mr. Daley's bird was biting the other bird's neck but he broke free. Then there was a pause while the birds seemed to flip back and right themselves. In a few seconds they were hurling at each other again. This time the other bird launched itself forward, feet first and its wings back. I saw the other rooster's gaff tear into the breast of Mr. Daley's bird and both were stuck together but they were still kicking and trying to fly. There was cheering and clapping for the other bird while Mr. Daley and the other owner ran over to untangle the roosters. The man pulled his bird off and there was blood on the gaff. Mr. Daley's bird seemed stunned and wobbled on its feet. Blood dripped from its chest. Someone yelled, "Clear the lungs, Earl." Mr. Daley knelt down and put his mouth to his bird's chest, sucked, and then spit blood. His lips and chin were smeared with red. He set his bird down on its shaky legs, but despite it being hurt, it flew again. The other rooster was quicker this time and dug its gaff deeper into the chest. Mr. Daley's rooster fell with the other bird on top. They were hooked together but one wasn't fighting. At that the owner ran into the ring and uncoupled the birds. He grabbed his rooster, raising it in the air while the men cheered.

Mr. Daley picked up his bird and cradled it in his arm, holding it like Mrs. Daley would one of her babies. He rubbed its back. Blood dripped to the dirt floor as he walked away, carrying it out the door. I hid behind a barrel of rancid water and watched him move toward his truck. He didn't put it in back with the two other roosters but reached through the open window, pulling a gunnysack from the seat. He wrapped it around the bird. Then he opened the door and got into the truck. I thought he'd leave but he didn't. He sat with his hands on the wheel and stared ahead. After a minute or so, he got out, slammed the door and strode back to get another bird.

That Monday when the school bus drove by I saw that the sign *ROOSTERS FOR SALE* had been taken down. When Elmer walked by me that morning, he had a black eye and his glasses were crooked with tape wrapped around the part that connects the bow to the frame.

I piped up, "Did you sell them all?" I wanted to tell him that I knew he didn't sell them because his daddy had them at the cockfight, but I held off.

He didn't say anything so I asked louder. "Did you?"

The other kids looked at me like I was crazy for talking to him, but I was intent on finding out all I could.

"Nope, didn't sell them."

The driver mumbled, "Are you the only one?"

Elmer nodded.

Then I noticed that Mr. Daley was in one of the pens with a rooster, feeding it. "Bet your daddy feels real bad about losing his good bird."

"He don't feel bad about nothing."

"Sure was a sad sight, seeing that one die," I said.

"How would you know?"

"I know more than you do." I puffed myself up so I sat a little higher.

"Doubt it," he said, not turning toward me.

I couldn't help but wonder if Elmer had gotten that black eye from his daddy. "Is Eustace sick?" I asked, turning around.

Elmer nodded but wouldn't say anything.

"Is he sick like you are?"

Elmer turned and looked at me with that weeping eye and said, "Just shut up."

But he didn't turn away from me so I softened my voice and asked, "Why do you and your brother's names start with *E*?"

"Because my momma liked it, I guess. All our names begin with *E*."

"Even your momma?"

"Yup, she's Elvira."

I felt like I was making some headway. "And your daddy's name is Earl. Right?"

He nodded.

"Bet he was mad that he lost one in that fight."

He glared at me and turned away.

I said quietly, my voice nice as pie, "When people get mad, sometimes they get real mean."

And Elmer's eyes teared up and he lifted the book higher so I couldn't see into them.

He wouldn't talk anymore.

That day at lunch I saw Eustace outside at the open cafeteria window. He was gesturing to Elmer to hurry over. Eustace looked a mess. His glasses were broken, too; one lens was cracked and I wondered how he'd be able to see with those cracks going right down through the middle. I couldn't tell if Eustace had a bruised cheek or if he was just dirty but his eye wasn't blackened like Elmer's. Maybe because he was bigger he could fight off his daddy, that's what I guessed. His tee shirt was dirty and dusty like he'd gotten caught in some windstorm. Eustace was whispering to Elmer and talking real quiet like he didn't want anyone to hear him. Next thing I knew Elmer was walking right out of the cafeteria door and heading to Mr. Daley's truck parked on the street. Eustace was driving but he wasn't very good at it. He had a hard time taking off; the truck jerked ahead like it just couldn't get enough gas to go anywhere. At that the principal walked over to the window to watch. Finally Eustace got it to move by gunning the engine and screeching the tires.

After school when the bus rounded the bend, I saw smoke where the roosters' shed used to be. It was now a pile of ashes. The wire pens were still there but the wire was black and melted together.

The rest of the kids on the bus flew to the windows. The bus driver slowed down.

They said, "Smells like fried chicken, don't you think?"

When I looked into the house, I saw Mrs. Daley in her rocker with her arm in a sling made from a white towel. Eustace was on the couch but I couldn't see Elmer. Something was different. There weren't any children in that living room.

The rest of us on the bus had rolled down the windows and had our heads and arms hanging out.

Someone said, "Look. There's feathers floating around the yard."

And sure enough, if we looked near the garage, there were feathers stuck to the bark of the ash tree and feathers on the gravel.

I wanted to go down to their place right away but Dad made me go with him to deliver a load of hay to a farmer up north. When I got home an hour later, I got on my bike. As I neared their place, I saw the sheriff's car parked in the yard and the sheriff was talking to Elvira who was standing on the back stoop. She had a bruised face and a fat lip. I stayed on the road and rode down further toward the bend and then turned around and headed back. I kept my eyes peeled. I saw the sheriff and Elvira near the burnt shed.

When I stopped my bike near the mailbox, Elmer was out on the step. That's when I noticed the truck was gone.

"What're you gawking at?" he yelled at me.

"Nothing," I said.

He came down the steps toward me. I didn't know whether to drive away or wait.

"You can't just sit there and watch us."

"Why not?" I said smartly.

"Because we have a right to privacy."

"Hey, this is a public road. I'm not coming into your yard."

"Well, get a move on it," he said. He was walking out that little bit of lane and heading to the mailbox.

I watched him open it and take out a catalog and a letter.

"Where's your daddy?" I asked.

"None of your beeswax," he answered.

"What kind of answer is that?"

Elmer looked at me. "My kind of answer."

I didn't say anything for a second. I let the silence hang there and Elmer didn't start walking back. He stood there with the mail in one hand and the other hand pushing up his broken glasses on his nose.

"How'd it burn down?" I asked quietly.

"Just used some gasoline and lit a match."

I was standing with my bike, my feet straddling it. "Was it your mom?"

He didn't answer.

"Did she do it because he hit you?"

"Hah, you think this is the first time? Naw, we've had beatings before. We're used to it. No, it's because he bought three more roosters with her money."

"I thought you were trying to get rid of them last week."

"Mom was. Dad wasn't."

Right then, we heard the sheriff call out, "Hey son, I need to talk to you."

Elmer looked at me sort of funny and said, "Want this catalog? It has all sorts of cheeses and meats in it. I never ordered anything but I would if I could. I'd get me that chocolate torte and a can of bear claws."

He handed it to me and turned to walk back to the sheriff who was walking over to him.

"Hey," I called out. "What's going on?"

Elmer shrugged as he kept on walking away from me. I saw his momma standing by the sheriff's car with her good hand at her neck, rubbing the flabby skin like she had worn something too tight.

I pushed my bike toward him and then remembered my manners, "Thanks for the catalog."

He paused and then turned and looked at me. "You know, you're the only school kid who's ever been to our place. When you stopped last week to buy the roosters, you weren't afraid to come into the yard. "

"Son, hurry up," said the sheriff.

He gave me a kind of nod and snorted the stuff in his nose into his throat.

I drove my bike a few yards down the road, just a little ways past a lilac bush, and then I stopped and stayed hidden.

I watched the sheriff handcuff Elmer and his momma and put

them in the back of the car. Then he went to the back door and knocked. But no one came out. He called in, "Eustace, no use trying to hide. We have to take you in."

That's when I noticed the deputy had gone around to the front door. The sheriff walked inside and a couple minutes later he was leading Eustace out in handcuffs. Eustace was crying and I saw that the lenses of his glasses were all foggy.

The sheriff's car drove away and next I saw another sheriff's car and an ambulance turn into the driveway. With shovels they dug through the rubble of the burnt chicken house. Underneath the pile of wire and boards they found Mr. Daley. After some more shoveling and moving of wood, they came out with his body covered in a gray blanket and put it in the ambulance.

That was the last I saw of them. And I felt bad about it. I felt bad even for the dad because a guy who holds a dead bird like it's a baby can't be too mean. And Elmer had been nice to me and I still have the catalog of cheeses and sausages and chocolates. At Thanksgiving I took my five dollars and twenty-eight cents and ordered a pound of bear claws and sent them to Elmer, who's at the State Training School for Boys in Eldora. You see, Elmer helped burn the pen down with his daddy in it and his daddy wasn't even dead yet—just knocked out with a hammer. Eustace did that. I guess their dad was putting up another divider for his new roosters and Eustace was telling him he shouldn't have spent the money, and then he hurled himself at his dad and knocked him down. Eustace just grabbed the hammer that was right there and whacked him a good one on the head. So that's why Eustace is at Cherokee in the crazy unit. He drug his old man into one of the pens with the new birds. I figured that Eustace went to get Elmer after it happened. The newspaper said Eustace confessed that the roosters had pecked his dad's eyes out and his lips were gone. And then their mom and Elmer started the fire to protect Eustace. That's why she's at Mitchellville, the women's prison.

When I filled out the catalog order, there was a place to write a few words. I thought and thought about what to write and couldn't come up with anything clever. I just said, "There's a lot more leftovers at lunch now that you're gone. The other day I was at the library and I found a book on Dr. Tom Dooley and I knew you'd read it because I saw jelly stains on the pages. Did you want to help people like he did?"

I got a letter back that said, "The bear claws were good. I ate them on Christmas Day. When I get out I'm going to go to baking school and learn how to make those. That's how I'm going to help people."

the Fogartys of the River Road

1961

*T*he Fogarty house was back from the road, hidden in a grove of trees and bushes, and eleven people lived there. The Fogartys had nine children. The parents were Chester and Eleanor, like Eleanor Roosevelt, and Chester on *Gunsmoke*. Chester wasn't much of a farmer but he sure was friendly. When he'd drive by our place he'd make a giant half circle, waving at me and Dad as if he hadn't seen us for years. He sat up on the John Deere seat like he was steering a ship.

The game warden was often parked at the end of their lane, afraid to drive in for fear of getting the belly of his car snarled with grass. But the warden wasn't there to see Chester. He was there to see John Francis, their oldest son, who was a hunter. He'd dropped out of school when he turned sixteen and the teachers were happy. He never looked them in the eye and never opened his mouth. People talked about seeing him leaning out of one of the upstairs windows with his gun. He shot anything that moved, but mostly he shot deer. Once he hung a couple racks of deer antlers above the front door. They were up there for a few weeks, then someone took them down. Dad said it wasn't deer-hunting season and that kid was just advertising his illegal hunting. John Francis had been fined twice last year for hunting out of season.

But what really advertised his hunting was his sister's new business of making moccasins. She began by putting a hand-painted sign up on the fence post that said: *Moccasins for Sale. Made with real deerskin by a real Indian.*

When the neighbors saw that, they began talking, not about the moccasins but about the real Indian part. It seemed Mrs. Fogarty, Eleanor, had half Indian blood in her, and she told people that she was related to Sacagawea, a Shoshone who traveled with Lewis and Clark, but no one really believed that part.

"She's just a Sioux," said Dad. "Maybe she's related to Inkpaduta but not Sacagawea." Dad had told me that Inkpaduta had camped below our farm on the river when he was on his way to the Spirit Lake Massacre.

Mary Kathleen could have been full-blooded Indian with her dark hair, eyes, and tan skin. I used to watch her as she got on the school bus each morning, looking so dull and scrubbed clean. By the time the bus got to school eight miles away, she was a different girl. She'd begin by tucking her blouse into her jeans, tightening the belt and rolling up the sleeves of the blouse so there was a cuff which showed off firm biceps. She'd unbutton the first three buttons and pull up the collar. Then she'd take a black pencil from her purse and using the mirror on her CoverGirl powder she'd draw a line around her eyes. Mascara was next, then an almost white lipstick, a frost with a hint of pink. And finally she'd take her brush and begin to rat her black hair all over. That hair grew and grew until it was three times its size. She'd brush the top layer over the ratted hair and pin a red bow in the hole between the bangs and the rest of the hair that she smoothed back away from her face. When she stood up to leave the bus that had stopped at the entrance to the high school, she swaggered. Finally I saw why. A young man was waiting for her at the bottom of the step. He threw his arm around her shoulder and led her to his car parked in the lot. And after school this transformation happened again when she was on her way home. Her boyfriend would watch her from his Chevy as she got on the bus. Once she sat down and waved to him, he'd squeal out right in front of the bus. The driver would shake his head and cuss a little under his breath. Then she'd take out a tissue, spit on it, and wipe everything off her face and comb through her hair until it was flat and hung down her back. She'd untuck her blouse and button up her shirt and would shuffle up the lane, looking at the ground. Sometimes John Francis was waiting for them at the side of the house. I thought he acted more like the dad. My dad usually waited for me to get off the bus when he wasn't helping out some farmer.

When most kids got on the bus they headed toward the back so they could talk without the driver hearing them, but not Mary Kathleen. She was always in the seat behind the driver, looking in the mirror and patting her hair. This routine went on for a few months until one morning in May she didn't fix her hair and makeup, and the young man wasn't waiting for her at the bottom step. Some of the big girls on the bus said something about her brother chasing her boyfriend away with a gun.

That summer I saw Mary Kathleen at the antique-car show selling moccasins. She had pulled back her black hair into a braid and had added a few feathers in back. She had a deerskin dress on as she stood behind her card table with a dozen pairs of moccasins. Her face was suntanned, without any makeup. And she appeared to be thicker all over, but it might have been the dress.

My dad and I had ridden into town in the pickup to see the cars. I don't know if Dad liked the car show, but he did it for me. It was something to do, something we could look at together and it was outside. My dad hated to do anything that was inside, anything that was confining. Dad did like going to the library, but only for an hour, no more. Each August when I had to shop for school clothes, he'd be jittery. He'd sit on a chair outside the dressing room at JC Penney's or Mary's Style Shop and wait for me while I tried on jeans and blouses. He'd never tell me to hurry up but his foot would be going up and down and his hands would be fidgeting. But if my dad was outside at the car show, he was content, unless there were a lot of people around.

In the middle of all the rows of cars was a section reserved for vendors selling food and trinkets. That's where I saw Mary Kathleen Fogarty with her wobbly card table. She looked strange, dressed in her deerskin next to church women in housedresses selling caramel corn and brownies at their long table. I noticed that she didn't talk to the other vendors and they didn't talk to her. Her moccasins were plain as could be. No beadwork on the toes, just tan deerskin with a brown shoelace running through so you could tighten it.

I walked up to the table and stood there. She didn't even try to give a sales pitch but looked out toward the rows of cars.

"Did you make them?" I asked her.

She didn't answer me, but nodded.

"You must get awful sore fingers trying to get a needle through that tough stuff." I touched one of the moccasins.

"I use a sewing machine."

"Do you get the skin from those deer your brother shoots?" I asked.

And I heard the ladies on either side of her begin to snicker and giggle. Mary Kathleen stared at me real hard, but she didn't say anything.

I had six dollars in my pocket and decided to buy a pair, mostly because I felt sorry for her. No one was hanging around buying her moccasins. I asked for my shoe size and she handed me a pair.

"Can I try them on?" I asked.

"If you get them dirty, you have to buy them."

So I sat down in the grass and was careful not to touch the ground when I put the moccasin on my right foot. The moccasin was too large. I tried three pairs before I found one that fit my foot. Then I noticed the stitching wasn't even and I knew it must have been one of her first efforts at being a shoemaker.

"Can I get this pair cheaper since it isn't made so good?" I asked.

"They're five dollars. And it's sewed to last."

"But the sewing's all crooked."

She reached out to grab the moccasin and I jumped back.

"I still want it," I said holding it to my chest. Two women came up and were looking at the table.

One lady whispered loud enough for us to hear. "I wouldn't get anything from a Fogarty. It'll probably fall apart as soon as you wear it."

And I saw Mary Kathleen's face harden and she stared out above their heads.

I waited until a few people had gone past when I said, "How did you get the fur off the skin?"

She scrunched her forehead and said, "What do you mean?"

"You know, how do you get the skin to be so soft?"

"We scrape the pelt and rub boiled deer brain on it and throw it in the ... " She didn't finish.

"Boiled deer brain. Why?"

"Because that's what the Indians did."

"And throw it in what?"

"Nothing. We just do it ourselves. Okay?"

"How long does it take?" I asked quietly, wondering if they chewed the skin like I had seen an Indian woman do in a movie.

She didn't answer me.

So I said it again. "How long does it take to the make this skin?"

"Why do you care?" she snarled. "Do you want those moccasins or not?"

I should have left them there and took off but I was too chicken to do anything. So I bought them for five dollars. It took me awhile to count out my change and I saw her moccasined foot tapping as I took my time. After I had the moccasins, which she didn't even put in a bag, I stood there looking at another pair.

"Just get out of here," she said.

She was checking the inside of each moccasin and I saw her take two pairs and put them in the suitcase under the table. I figured that they must have really been sewed sloppily.

Just then her brother, John Francis, came walking up to the table.

He was also dressed in buckskin like he was a mountain man. He carried a muzzleloader over his shoulder and announced to her, "Just sold my last piece of jerky."

She looked at him and then made a face toward me and rolled her eyes. He stopped and studied me and I felt scared. I took off out of there ready to find my dad.

On the way home I told Dad about the poor stitching in some of the moccasins and he said, "You stay away from them. They're nothing but con artists. They take after their dad."

"What'd he do?"

"He grows funny weeds and sells them," he said, acting like I didn't know what he was talking about.

"You mean marijuana?" I asked.

Dad rubbed his chin. "How do you know about that?"

"The older kids tell us about that stuff at school."

Dad whistled and looked angry. "Damnnation!" he said. "Well, you stay away from that Fogarty outfit. Something's not right with those guys."

"Like what?" I pressed.

"Like they aren't normal. Too many younguns and Eleanor's way past her prime." And then my dad realized that he was saying too much, so he clamped his mouth shut.

But that was just the beginning of our association with the Fogartys. In July Dad got a call from Chester about doing some baling for him. Dad didn't want to do it because Chester's field was full of weeds that clogged up the baler and it had lots of rocks in it. So my dad thought he had a good excuse by saying, "Can't get the baler down to the river bottom without damaging it."

"The road's better this year. John Francis has been using it."

"No, can't take the risk of another breakdown. That's my bread and butter. Can't do it."

My dad thought that was the end of it but Chester drove into our lane a day later. He had five kids in the back of his truck. There were three black-haired ones and two redheads. The redheads, who were in the grade above me, got their hair color from Chester. Chester got out of the truck and walked to where my dad was fixing the baler. This time he had a fistful of bills and handed them to Dad. I saw a couple of fives and tens and a twenty. He was offering him cash before he even began. No one did this. They waited until the bales were in the barn and sometimes they waited a few more days before they brought over the money. I was used to this. Dad and I went grocery shopping on those days when he got paid. And sometimes we'd go to the Farm and Home Store and get twine for the baler or a pitchfork or some worm medicine for Buster, our dog.

When I watched from the machine shed, I saw Dad hesitate a second and then he took the money. I'm sure he took it because Chester hadn't paid him enough last year when he baled. The agreement was made with a few nods and a handshake. Dad still held the wad of bills when Chester drove away with the kids squealing and fighting in the back of the truck. I saw one dark-haired girl who couldn't have been more than three years old holding onto the side of the rack.

The next morning after the dew was off the fields, we headed down the river road. Dad was on the tractor and I was on the flatbed, my feet apart, leaning against the back rack. I held my breath as Dad slowly made his way into their long lane. Everywhere I looked there was something out of place. I saw a mixing bowl near a tree, a red plastic pitcher in the grass, a car tire on the ground leaning against a pitchfork with a broken tine, a one-tired bike leaning against a tree, and a pile of wet newspapers near a shed. In a clearing, a few barrels were smoking from the trash burning in them. They could stand to burn more. And then I saw Mary Kathleen, barelegged in a man-sized shirt covering a basketball belly, standing in front of the back door, or what was left of the back door. The screen was out and the door was off its hinges so it stayed open all the time. A storm door with broken glass was closed. Plastic covered the glass part.

She was smoking a cigarette like she did it all the time. And then her momma came out and took the cigarette from her hand and took a puff. It was like they were sharing something special and they seemed real close. And for a second I was envious of them and would have given anything to have been in their place. They just stood there side by side and watched us and then looked over us toward the bottomlands. And I thought how they had a nice view from where they were. The river below them moved slowly in its snakelike channel. It was low this time of year and it seemed to have no energy to go anywhere.

The little girl who had been in the back of the truck ran up to Mary Kathleen and threw her arms around her knees. She leaned her head into the part below her stomach like she was used to doing it all the time. And Mary Kathleen paid no mind to her but just let her root into that warm place until she got tired of it. Then the mom pulled out a handkerchief and put it to the girl's nose. The girl blew, and she took off for the oak tree where the drooping bag swing, made from a gunny sack stuffed with straw, was hanging.

John Francis and two red-haired brothers named Angus and Alroy stacked the bales on the wagon. Both Angus and Alroy were in eighth grade but Alroy was repeating it. Chester and Mary Kathleen and three younger ones unloaded the wagon and put the bales on the ground near the barn, not inside the barn as normal farmers do. I wondered if Mary Kathleen should be lifting those heavy bales but no one seemed to be worried about it. Even Eleanor came out to help, but she was having a difficult time. I tried to give them a hand, too, but they didn't seem too interested in me. So I took off to wander around that yard. I kept thinking that this place was like one of those find-what's-hidden-in-the-picture puzzles that Miss Blankenship lets us do when we've finished our homework. I love searching for bananas, hammers, and sailboats in a jungle.

Near the barn I stepped on a fly swatter. It was one that was given away at the county fair by the fertilizer company. Dad kept ours on a nail near the stove. When I got to the barn, I tried to pull open the door but it was locked. I tried another door and that was locked also.

That's when Mary Kathleen came over and said, "What are you doing?"

"Just wanted to see what was in the barn. You should put the bales in there. They need to be dry, you know."

"We'll put tarps over them."

Mary Kathleen pulled on the door and it wouldn't give. She seemed satisfied that it was locked.

"What do you have in there?" I asked, motioning toward the barn.

"None of your business," she answered.

"My dad said I could play here while he finished with the field."

She sneered at me. "Go on home and leave us alone."

Her stomach was sticking way out and it looked hard. She put her hand to the small of her back like it hurt her and leaned back. That's when I got brave and said, "Pretty soon, huh?"

She seemed stunned. "What are you talking about?"

"Your baby. Must be getting ready to come out pretty soon?"

I waited for her to snarl at me again, but she was quiet. Then she said, "I guess it'll come out when it's ready."

"When does the doctor say it's supposed to come?" I kept my voice nice as pie.

"What doctor?" she said. "We can't afford one."

"But where will you go to have it?"

She laughed. "Nowhere. I'll have it right here."

I kept pressing. "But who will pull it out? Who will do what the doctor does?"

"My, you're snoopy," she said, and as if realizing she had said too much, she turned away.

I walked out that weedy lane and started down the road. But once I got past the grove of trees and shrubs, I stopped adjacent to a cornfield. I went into the ditch and up over a fence and into the cornfield and came out behind the grove.

I bided my time until the next load of straw came in. When everyone was busy unloading, I worked my way through the grove, cussing them for never clearing it out and for raising a nest of mosquitoes, which bit me to no end. I kept to the back of the barn and worked my way to the old cellar in the bottom.

Sure enough, there were slits between the boards and the foundation and I peeked in. That's when I saw two large wooden barrels. A tarp was over the top of one.

Three hides were stretched along the barn walls, fastened with nails. Two hides were drying on a rope clothesline and they looked rather stiff, not the soft doeskin of those moccasins. There must be another process that they had to go through. I wondered if John Francis had to pound them to make them soft.

I worked my way to the door that had a padlock on it and I gave it a pull. Nothing. Then I began searching the outside of the building for a key. I knew farmers. There'd be a key somewhere because if they were like my dad he'd lose it if he kept it in his jeans pocket. I kept my eyes peeled and ran my hands along the rock foundation. Then I saw it. On a nail behind some wild grape vines was the key. The padlock opened easily and I left the key in the padlock. I stepped inside. I pulled my shirt up to my nose and covered it. The smell was awful, like a mixture of hard-boiled eggs, vinegar, and battery acid. Both barrels were set on gray block probably so they wouldn't tip. The barn floor was dirt packed and uneven. As I walked around I looked up and saw deer heads with empty eyes hanging from nails about eight feet from the floor. I counted twenty-eight heads of all sizes—from fawns to eighteen-point stags. John Francis must have been busy. I saw a brick near one of the wooden barrels and I guessed it was used by John Francis like a footstool. He'd step on it when dropping things into the barrel.

I felt an eerie sense of being watched by the ghosts of all these dead deer. They were blind—no eyes—since the eyes had dried up, but I felt they were still looking at me. Flies buzzed around the barn and it looked like some had eaten away at the fur on many of the heads.

I stepped up on the brick. The green tarp was old and holey. I picked it up and almost lost my balance when the smell coming out from under the tarp hit me. It was hard to see what was in the wooden barrel because it was so dark. The liquid was dark, black. Even with squinting I could see nothing. But I suddenly felt a chill seeing bubbles, and something furry and round floated up to the surface. I thought it was a deer head with eyes looking at me.

Then I heard the squeak from the door. "Get the hell away from there," she said. Mary Kathleen was standing there with her hand holding the door open so sunlight came in and exposed me. I didn't say a word but stepped down from the brick, my legs shaking. There was no other way out but past her.

When I got even with her, I felt her hands on my blouse. "John Francis is going to be burning mad that you were in here. And if you tell anyone and that game warden comes around, we'll know who to get."

"I didn't do anything."

Mary Kathleen's stomach was touching me. She was out of breath and struggling to hold onto me with her hands. "You shut the hell up. If you tell anyone, even your daddy, then . . . " She motioned to the tanks and I saw her nod her head. "In there. That's where you'll end up."

And I felt myself get sick. My breakfast cereal came erupting out of me and she jumped back and screamed while I threw up at her feet.

I didn't tell my dad, but I couldn't get her threat out of my mind. I rode my bike down the road almost every day to see if I'd get a glimpse of Mary Kathleen. About two weeks later I saw a couple of the younger ones hanging out by the closed gate to the lane. There were sheep in the yard so Chester must have borrowed some from a neighbor to mow the lawn.

I stopped my bike on the road and nodded.

The eight-year-old black-haired girl yelled, "How come you're always riding by here?"

"I like to ride by. It's a public road." That seemed to be my answer. I gave that same one to the Daley boys last year.

"My big sister says to watch out for you because you're a snoop. She says to not let you onto our place," the red-haired ten-year-old said.

"I don't want to go in there," I said. "Your place is too messy."

The dark-haired girl whispered something to this girl. Then they both giggled and I felt strange having two girls laugh at me.

"What are you laughing about?" I asked.

"Nothing."

"Why are you hanging out here?"

The black-haired one said, "Because they won't let us in the house."

"Why not?"

I saw the red-haired girl hit the other girl and say, "Be quiet."

"I didn't say anything, Mary Carolyn," she shot back.

"Didn't say what?" I asked.

There was silence and I looked down the lane and saw the rest of the kids were all in the yard. Even Chester was leaning against the front of the old Buick, smoking.

"How come everyone's outside?"

The tiny black-haired one that had been in the back of the truck the day they stopped in our place stepped out from behind Mary Carolyn. "Because my mom's having a baby."

I had guessed it. She was Mary Kathleen's daughter. I added up the years. She was three years old and Mary Kathleen was maybe fifteen so she'd had her when she was twelve.

Mary Carolyn kicked her for talking and she started crying. At that Angus came walking out toward them and I debated about leaving. But I held to my spot on the road.

"Hey you, skedaddle on home."

I knew Angus from school. He was a year ahead of me in eighth grade and I always felt bad for him because he never had his homework done. I'd heard the teachers talking in the office one time when I was waiting for my dad to pick me up for a dentist's appointment. They were complaining about the family and that they seemed to have some problem where they couldn't learn.

"How long has she been in there?" I motioned to the house.

"What?"

"How long has she been trying to get that baby out?"

"Since last night. She's moaning and Mom keeps telling Dad that we have to get her to the hospital but he won't take her. Says he doesn't want them social workers coming out here."

As we stood there, we heard a long scream coming from the
house and we all turned. We listened and it happened again. Another
scream. I stood there until the creamery truck came by and I had to
get over to the side of the road.

"Gosh, maybe you should get her to town. Seems like she's in pain."

"Ah, Dad says that's just how it is with women birthing,"
said Angus.

I waited a little while longer and heard a few more screams
and then I took off. Dad would be looking for me.

Toward evening I rode my bike down the road and stopped
at the cornfield behind their grove. I left my bike in the ditch and
walked through the field. I had worn a long-sleeved shirt and jeans
to keep the mosquitoes from biting me. I made my way into the grove,
staying behind the biggest trees. After what seemed like an hour, I saw
Eleanor carrying a pile of newspapers and a bloody sheet out to the
barrel. She took a match and lit the end of the sheet but it went out as
soon as she left. The blood looked new and red. It was too wet to burn.
Things were real quiet and I figured that meant it was all over. She
must have had the baby.

I told my dad about the baby and the newspaper, but I didn't
tell him about the bloody sheets. Somehow I knew that that was not
okay to talk about with a man. I kept thinking that she must have
had her period about the same time she had the baby. I knew about
periods from my friend Janice, but I didn't know much about babies.
That was coming up this year in seventh grade home economics class.
Sometimes I missed having a mom and even having a mom like Mary
Kathleen was better than nothing.

For the next week I watched the house hoping to see Mary
Kathleen with a baby but I didn't. Once I saw her at the front door
smoking and she was skinny again.

When school started two weeks later, she wasn't waiting at the
end of the lane. For two days I waited to see her but she wasn't there.
Finally on the third day I asked Angus, "Where's your big sister?"

"She's through with school. Turned sixteen this summer so she can quit. Next year I'll be able to quit, too."

"You'll be sixteen?" I asked. "But you're only in eighth grade."

He turned red and scowled at me.

"I suppose she's home with her baby," I said.

He didn't answer me but hurried to the back seat.

Later that day after school, I sat in front of Mary Carolyn. "How's the new baby?" I asked, trying to be friendly.

She didn't answer me.

I kept going. "Bet it's fun to have a little one around. I wish I had a little baby sister." I paused. "Is it a girl or boy?"

Mary Carolyn kept looking away from me and out the window.

I became more persistent. "Is it a girl or boy?"

"A girl," she whispered.

"What did you name her?"

Mary Carolyn looked at me with angry eyes. "Will you shut up," she said.

I was surprised by her reaction. "I'm not trying to make you mad. I just wanted to be friendly."

"Well, we don't have to talk to you. Dad says to not tell you nothing." And she got up and moved to the last seat to sit with Angus and Alroy.

I was real upset because her dad had said that about me. What had I done to them? That evening while Dad and I were making our usual Tuesday night goulash with some sliced tomatoes on the side, I told him about my conversation with Mary Carolyn and Angus.

"Don't you think it's strange that they won't tell me its name?"

"Maybe they don't want people to know much. You know, they might be ashamed that she had a baby so young."

"But Dad, she had one a couple years ago. That dark-haired girl is hers, too."

Dad looked at me with a wrinkled forehead. "How do you know that?"

"I know. I've seen her with Mary Kathleen. I can tell by that way they act that she's the mother. You know, Dad, it's real obvious."

He lifted his eyebrow and said, "How is it?"

"Well, she rubs her head against her and hangs on her legs. And she looks just like her but then she looks like her older brother, too."

Dad set the fry pan right on the table, but he put a hot pad underneath it. He said it was called a skillet casserole and that meant we could eat right out of it. He said, "I told you to stay away from them and I mean it. They're strange folk."

"They're strange all right. They can't even tell you the name of a baby. Maybe they haven't even named it yet."

Dad scooped up a big spoonful and put it on my plate. I liked goulash, especially when Dad put in more hamburger and macaroni and less carrots.

The next Saturday afternoon I saw the Fogartys in the bottomland digging out potatoes and carrots for winter. I followed my usual path through the dried cornfield that would be harvested soon, through the grove and up to the house. I peeked in the window to the kitchen and saw jars of canned things all over the counter and table. Then I went to another window and saw the living room with a davenport with some kind of blanket on it, a wood rocking chair, pots and pans and a full clothesbasket, two dolls on the floor and a color TV. The floor was linoleum and the walls were a dark green color. A crucifix was hanging above the TV. It was a mess just like I expected. I wanted one of those color TVs but Dad wouldn't get it. Instead we had our old twelve-inch black and white.

I didn't see anyone.

That's when I decided to try the barn. Pushing through the weeds, I made my way down the hill, hearing the music getting louder. I stayed in the tall ironweeds and waited. The door was open. The music was crackling and I figured it was a radio that needed an antenna. In a way I was happy there was a radio because it covered up any noise I made.

Carefully, I moved closer to the spot where I knew I could see. I looked through the crack and saw Mary Kathleen at a table scraping a hide. It looked like a fresh hide because I saw lots of flies and gooey bloody junk on the edges. She was skinny and bent over and I thought she could pass for a much older lady. She had an old flannel shirt on and jeans. Her hair was pulled back in a ponytail. Maybe that was it. She didn't look like the girl on the bus with the ratted hair. I looked around for a place she'd keep a baby but there was nothing. The radio was on a window ledge and it was plugged into an extension cord that went up through the ceiling to the top floor. The window was dirty but still some light came through it. It was bright enough so she could see what she was doing.

She held a tool that looked like a blade of a knife and she was scraping it back and forth, the fur falling to the dirt floor. Her tennis shoes were covered in deer fur and she didn't even notice. Then I was surprised to see John Francis coming from the top of the barn, climbing down a ladder. His clothes were dirty and stained.

He walked over to Mary Kathleen and leaned over to look at her and she turned away from him. Then he moved closer to get his face in hers again and she turned away. At that he walked behind her and put his hands on her shoulder and she shrugged him off. He backed off and then came toward her again and hit her shoulder with his hand. She threw down the blade and stood up and walked toward me.

I raced toward the weeds and flattened myself.

"Stay away," she called out.

And I could hear her moving near me but I held my breath.

I then heard him yell. "Get back here and do this. It has to be done now."

"Fuck you," she called out.

I waited with my head down for five minutes. When I felt like she was gone and he was back in the barn, I climbed up that slope and took off toward the grove. I made my way through the bushes and finally out to the cornfield. It was always a relief to hit the field, which was safe territory. I found my bike in the ditch and pulled it toward the road. That's when I saw Mary Kathleen ahead of me, walking down the road like she was trying to get away.

I guessed she hadn't seen my bike in the ditch. The long grass had concealed it. I decided to follow her, to get my chance to talk to her. When I got closer to her, I saw that her hands were all red and stained.

"Hey," I said as I made my way around her.

She looked like she'd been crying and she kept her head down.

"Nice day isn't it?" I said.

She didn't say anything.

I stopped in front of her and decided I had to take a chance. "Heard you have a baby girl," I said.

Her eyes darkened. "Who said that?"

"Your sister told me. On the bus. But she didn't tell me her name. What did you name her?"

She looked like her wind had been knocked out of her. She stopped and kicked at the gravel.

"Did you name her Mary something, like your name?" I asked.

She lifted her head and looked at me. "No, her name was Kimberly."

I felt that something was wrong. I had heard the word *was* and I wondered if I should ask. But I didn't say a word.

She had a faraway look on her face and didn't seem to care that her hands were stained. "Kimberly. It's a pretty name, don't you think?"

She was asking someone who wasn't there. I mean she looked at me but she wasn't seeing me. I saw someone real confused and sick.

I answered, "Yes, it's a real pretty name."

And then she started moving again, heading down the road toward my farm. I followed at a distance and watched her walk right by our lane.

I found Dad in the machine shed fixing the combine. He was already combining beans for folks. When I told Dad about Mary Kathleen and how weird she was acting, he perked up. He walked to the end of our lane and watched her. She was about a quarter mile from our lane and still moving. She'd reach the highway soon.

"Shouldn't we do something?" I said.

"What can we do? She's just walking. She didn't break the law."

"But Dad, she said 'was.' That means that baby isn't alive. What happened to it?"

I wouldn't quit so my dad called the sheriff who had an acreage near town. Dad had baled for him in July and was on friendly terms with him.

I don't know what Dad told him but later that day two sheriff cars were parked at the end of the Fogarty lane. The next day on the radio the announcer said that Mary Kathleen was picked up hitchhiking near St. Cloud. She was agitated and incoherent. She was taken in and that was when it all came out.

For a week the sheriff and his deputies and the Division of Criminal Investigation were all over that farm. Soon the lane didn't have any weeds in the middle track. It was clean from all the wear and tear. They finally found the baby in the bottom of the tank of tanning fluid. She was wonderfully preserved. A pretty baby. Some say it was born dead and John Francis was supposed to have buried it but instead he tied a brick to it and sent it to the bottom of the tank. I heard my dad say that some folks thought it was John Francis's baby, or Chester's, and others thought it belonged to the guy who owned the Chevy.

Dad says we just don't have much luck with neighbors and he's thinking of moving to town so I can be around normal people. Eleanor and Chester moved to Missouri after losing most of their kids and grandkids. Seems like no one was sure how many children John Francis had fathered and how many Chester had. No one was talking much. All the little kids were sent to foster homes. And Mary Kathleen walked out of jail after John Francis confessed and she kept walking north and no one knows where she went. But I think of her when I drive by her place and see that the weeds in the lane have grown up bigger than ever, and when I wear my moccasins I wonder what happened to all those other pairs she'd made and never had a chance to sell. And Dad says the deer are back. He saw three standing near the Fogarty's barn.

the
Kitchen
band :part I

1962

*B*efore my mom left us, she was in
the kitchen band for a short time. Now, how did anyone ever talk her
into dressing up in a housedress with an apron and wearing on her
head a basket decorated with copper scrub pads that were supposed
to look like flowers? In the photo my mom is the youngest one in
the group. The other women all seem to be in their fifties or sixties.
Sometimes I want to tell Dad that maybe that drove her away—
playing in the band with all those old ladies. But I know it's not the
real reason. I think it was Dad and me—we were too much for her,
along with the farm and losing her job at the bar in town and drinking
too much. I know my mom drank from clear tall bottles because I
found a couple of them after she left. One was behind the Christmas
box in the basement and another was in the cupboard where we kept
the waffle iron and Christmas cookie cutters—things we didn't use
much at all. When I showed them to Dad he got mad and poured the
liquid down the sink like he was punishing it.

But the kitchen band photo that I have hanging on my wall in
my bedroom seems so out of place with my posters and stuff and the

things I have from my mom. I didn't always have that photo.
I happened onto it when I was helping Clare clean one day. Clare
lives about three miles from us to the north and she was having a
rough time with her broken leg. So Dad volunteered me to help her
twice a week. I was to wash her dishes and clothes and run up and
down her stairs taking things back and forth.

I was dusting the top of her piano, lifting stacks of books and
sheet music when I saw the corner of it. It was underneath a piece
of sheet music that said "Beer Barrel Polka." The name sounded funny
and didn't seem like Clare, who was a lady who wouldn't drink beer,
maybe wine. Dad said she was a college-educated woman who for
years taught voice and piano lessons and French at the high school,
that is until they got rid of French because only three students signed
up for it. I saw the edge of the photo with a lady wearing a plastic
pitcher on her head and holding a breadboard and a wooden spoon.
When I pulled it out, I asked Clare. "What's this?"

I held it up for her to see. And she told me it was the kitchen band
that had played at weddings and parties for a few years. I was almost
ready to put it back when she asked in a softer voice, "Recognize
anyone?"

I looked again and then I saw her. I walked over to Clare and
pointed at the young woman in the back row.

She nodded and said, "Your mom."

"Her hair is up on her head. I thought she always wore it down?"

"Not that day. It was hot and she wanted it off her neck."

"Where was it taken?"

Clare shifted herself on the couch to get comfortable. "At the
state fair. It was over one hundred degrees that day. We won a blue
ribbon in the talent contest."

I stood there holding that photo and looking at my mom. "I can't
believe Mom would want to be in this kind of band."

Clare laughed. "She didn't. Myrna got sick and we were supposed
to have fourteen ladies in the band because that's what we said we'd
have on our registration form. So I asked your mom. I think she did

it because she got to go to Des Moines for the weekend."

"How old was I?"

"Oh, maybe four or five."

"Did Dad and me go along?"

"No, she went with us ladies."

I leaned closer, my head only two inches away from the photo, and asked, "How soon after this did she leave?"

Clare was quiet. "Oh, I don't know exactly. It was shortly after, I think. Can you ask your dad?"

"Dad doesn't like to talk about it much."

"I'm sure it's too hard for him," Clare answered.

"Do you remember much about this day? Was she excited to be there?"

Clare cleared her throat. "She didn't like wearing that dress and apron. She wanted to be in the back row so she could hide. I do remember that."

I put the photo back on the piano but this time on top of the stack of music. All that morning I kept looking at the photo until Clare told me I could take it home if I promised to bring it back sometime. She had only one copy of it.

So I took it home. I didn't say anything to my dad for a few days. I wanted to keep the photo to myself while I studied it. I could tell every detail about Mom from that photo. She had hoop earrings and a big ring on her finger—like one of those turquoise rings you buy from vendors at the fair. I didn't remember seeing that ring in her wooden jewelry box. She left her wedding ring in that box but not this ring.

When I showed this photo to my dad, he seemed surprised. He said he'd never seen it before, that this was taken a month before she ran away. I questioned him about that weekend and he said she'd been mad at him and had done this just to get away and to make him madder. He said when she came back she was moody and tired. He said he couldn't imagine that all those women stayed out late at night but Mom must have. She slept for two days and was sick.

That's when I knew I had something important in my hand.

When I was dusting end tables at Clare's again, I asked her.

"Who did my mom sleep with on the trip? I mean, did she share a room with some other ladies?"

"Of course she did. We had to sleep two to a bed, four to a room. We didn't have much money."

"Who were the three other women with her?"

Clare looked at the photo I'd brought along with me and told me that Hilda Jenson was one of them but she couldn't remember the other two.

When I asked where Hilda lived, she said, "In town now. After Hank died she moved to town and lives right near the Catholic church."

On Saturday I went with Dad to town. For once, I was happy my teacher had assigned me to write a memoir. Now I knew what I was going to do. I told Dad I needed to be at the library for two hours to work so he could pick me up later. I had looked in the phone book earlier and memorized the address. I still had the photo with me.

I found my way from the library to the church and to her house. When Hilda answered the door, she seemed scared or confused to see me. I introduced myself and told her Clare gave me her name. Then I showed her the photo and said I wanted to know about that weekend and my mom because I was writing a memoir for English. I was supposed to interview people as part of the project. English teachers were big on interviewing. Last fall in seventh grade we'd had to interview people who lived during the Depression. Every old person in town had kids with tape recorders visiting them. In fact, the teacher had given the editor some of the good ones and they were printed in the *Emmetsburg Reporter*.

Hilda, who had worn a lampshade hat in the kitchen band, walked with a cane and led me to her living room. I sat on one of the green recliners and she sat on the other one. They looked just like the ones I'd seen in the Sears catalog, except hers were worn.

"My mom shared a room with you when you went to the state fair. What do you remember about her and the weekend?"

"We didn't see much of her. She took off on her own. She said she was meeting some friends at the midway. And she didn't come in until late at night. We were worried about her."

"Why?"

"Well, you know, it was a big place and there were all kinds of riffraff at the fair. We didn't want her to get lost and forget to show up for the talent show. She was almost late, you know."

"Really. How late?"

"We were to play at two, or was it three? Anyway she was supposed to be back at our room at noon to get ready. I don't remember much but you know who would? Gladys Timmons. I think she was the one who took her dress and hat and instrument along in the car. There was something about leaving a note and having your mom meet us at the pavilion."

"Is Gladys alive?"

"Heavens, yes. She's my neighbor. Let me call her up and tell her to come over."

And that's how I ended up meeting Gladys, the one who wore a plate-and-coffee-cup hat. She came in the back door wearing a pair of overalls and muddy shoes, which she took off at the kitchen door. She walked in white stocking feet into the living room.

"You were lucky to catch me. I just stepped inside to go to the bathroom. Been in the garden breaking up the dirt," she said.

Hilda introduced her to me and Gladys seemed confused, like she couldn't figure out what I wanted to know.

"She's writing a paper for English. Wants to know about the kitchen band and her mom." Hilda was talking loudly into Gladys's ear.

"What band?" Gladys asked.

"Show her the photo," Hilda said to me.

And I handed the photo to her and her face lit up. "Our kitchen band. What about it?"

I jumped in. "My mom was in it. I want to know about her."

Gladys took off her glasses and held the photo close to her eyes. "Why haven't I seen this before?"

Hilda shook her head and raised her eyes at me. "Gladys, you've seen it. We passed it around at Good Neighbor Club a couple of months after the fair."

"I must not have been there because I ain't seen this until now." Gladys kept that photo in front of her for a good three minutes. Finally she said, "We were a good-looking group, weren't we? My, we had fun. Too bad it fell apart."

"How did it?" I asked.

"What?" Hilda asked.

"Why did it fall apart?"

"Because Clare got too busy at school and didn't have time for us." Gladys's voice was bitter.

"Now, don't be so mean. She was busy. Had to take over for that vocal music teacher who quit in the middle of the year."

"Well, when summer came she could have started it back up."

Hilda glanced at me and smiled. "She got sick, remember? Spent most of the summer in bed with that infection."

"She thought we weren't good enough for her. She was always yelling at us to stay with the beat and to do this and that."

"Gladys, I didn't bring you over here to air our dirty laundry about the band. I wanted you to tell her about her mom. You remember Lisa. We shared a room with her."

At that Gladys looked at the photo again. "Oh, I remember all right. But I don't think you want to know."

"What do you mean?"

"Just leave it alone. She wasn't really one of us. We just needed her to fill in for Myrna when she had her hysterectomy. She only practiced a few times with us."

"In writing a memoir we must risk telling the unpleasant," I said. "That's what our teacher says. So I can handle what you tell me."

"Well, she just about got us disqualified because she was almost late. I had her dress and hat and tambourine but I didn't have her apron. She had to run back to the hotel to get it. And she went with some tough-looking carni ... "

I saw Hilda kick Gladys and she stopped.

"Who was she with?" I asked.

"Nothing. She got a ride with someone she met at the fair."

"Who was it?"

"It doesn't matter. But she made it back about two minutes before we were going on. We were mad at her. She could have gotten us disqualified. And she didn't even apologize for it. No, you and your dad are better off without her."

"Gladys," Hilda warned.

"Well, they are. She wasn't much …"

Hilda jumped in. "She did a fine job for having only two practices with us. And we won a blue ribbon."

"But you said she went to meet her friends at the midway. Did you see her with any of these friends?"

Gladys crossed her arms and cleared her throat. "Nope. I only know that she stayed out plenty late and was throwing up in the toilet when I got up at five."

"Did you ask her what was wrong?" I asked. "Did she have the flu?"

"Honey, she had the brown-bottle flu, that's what she had. Oh my, and she smelled like a brewery."

Hilda tried to soften things. "She might have had a touch of sun stroke. Folks were getting sick from it."

"Good Lord, Hilda. I smelled beer, not suntan lotion."

I wondered if everyone knew about my mom but me. Did she drink all the time? I wondered if she lost her job at the tavern because she was drinking too much.

"Did she go to bed?" I asked.

"Yup, crawled into bed looking like a drowned rat. Hair all damp and messed up like it had never seen a comb."

Hilda said, "Well, she had it combed for the performance."

"Did not. She just pulled it up on her head with some leather hair thingamajig."

"I remember Bea putting some rouge on her cheeks to perk her up some."

Gladys smiled. "She was a sassy thing, that's for sure. Came flying in there late. We had to dress her almost. Then she slapped the lipstick out of Bea's hand when she tried to put it on her when we were backstage."

And Hilda added, "Remember how it rolled out onto the stage?"

"Sure do. That was when those tap dancing twins were doing that God-awful routine. We got to laughing because we thought they might step on it."

"Bea picked it up when we went on stage to play. That lipstick rolled around half stuck out and it didn't break off."

"How did my mom get to the place if you guys were all there ahead of time?"

"Like I said, some riffra …"

Hilda softened it. "Some friend she met."

I asked, "What did she do after you won? Did you all go out to celebrate?"

Gladys pushed her shirt down into the overalls. "Oh, she celebrated but not with us. We saw her later that night when we were walking around the fairgrounds—after it cooled off—and she wasn't feeling any pain, let me tell you. Hanging on that guy again and he taking liberties that he shouldn't be taking with a married woman …"

"Gladys, enough. She wants to know the good things about her mom."

"Well, there ain't much good to tell, dammit."

I stood up ashamed and embarrassed. This was my mom they were talking about. "I have to go back to the library to meet my dad. I can't be late."

"Are you going to walk?" Hilda asked.

"Yes," I answered.

"Let me give you a ride," Hilda offered.

"No, let me. Hilda, you're not moving too fast with that leg. I'll give her a ride."

When I tried to insist that I could walk, Gladys just grabbed my elbow and pushed me toward the door. She put on her boots and we walked out the back and across the yard to her yard and into her garage where there was a green Chrysler parked. I got in the passenger's side and she got in the driver's side. The keys were already there.

I felt scared being with this big lady who wore overalls like she was born in them. She had dark skin with lots of wrinkles like she'd spent a lot of time in the sun.

When she turned the corner onto the library street, she said to me, "I don't think you need to write that stuff I told you about your mom. Just write that she helped us win the blue ribbon. That's all you need."

"I don't know what I'll write. But I'm glad you told me what you did, even though I wished it could have been different. I guess now I understand why she ran away."

Gladys pulled into a spot in front of the library and put the car in park. "You do, huh. Let's hear what you think."

"Well, I guess she had another boyfriend, the guy she met at the fair, and he probably came for her. Took her away."

"That might be right. Someone said they saw that carnival guy at the Spencer fair a month later. And I know your mom got a ride over to the fair with Clem Molloy and that was the last we ever saw of her. Except Bea saw her one time in Florida when she wintered down there."

"Who's this Bea?"

"You know, Bea Kibbie. She used to work in the bank but she's retired. Volunteers at the library, shelving books. You might find her there sometime. She has dyed black, frizzy hair. And has her glasses hanging from a gold chain. I don't know why she just can't leave those glasses on her face where they belong."

I saw my dad parked across the street waiting for me. I got out of the car and hurried over to him.

"Where have you been? The librarian said you left an hour ago. What's going on? And what in Sam Hill are you doing with Gladys?"

Dad's neck was stretched tight so I knew he was really mad.

"I'm working on a memoir for English."

"And ..."

"And I was interviewing Gladys."

"Why Gladys?"

"Because she was in the kitchen band with Mom."

Dad took a deep breath of air and shot it out like it was burning his belly. "Leave it alone, can't you? Ever since you found that damn picture that's all you do is look at it."

"That's because I want to know about her."

"Well, she doesn't want to know about you."

I felt the barb of those words as my eyes teared up. "Maybe if you'd loved her more and been nicer to her, maybe she wouldn't have left," I said.

"You don't know what you're talking about. She left because she hated the farm and everything connected with it."

"And maybe you don't know what you are talking about." He didn't know about the man she'd met in Des Moines and I wasn't sure if I should tell him. But right then I wanted to blurt it out and hurt him some more.

"What do you mean?"

"Nothing. Nothing."

"Come on. . . . What did you mean? What did Gladys tell you?"

"She just told me about Mom not liking that dress and apron and how she really didn't like being in the band at all."

"Well, I could have told you that. She just did it because it was so off the wall—you know, a gag."

"I think some of them thought she did it to help out," I said.

"I don't think she cared much for those ladies. She wasn't a do-gooder, if you know what I mean. She was out for herself."

"You can't say one good thing about her, can you?"

"Nope, I can't. And just remember, dammit, that I've raised you, not her."

"Dad, I know you raised me. And I'm not going to leave but I do want to find out more about her, and you won't tell me a thing."

"I don't talk about her because I'm still so mad at her. I wish she were dead. It would be easier to deal with her."

"Why don't you divorce her? End it."

"I just don't want to think about it. I don't want to dredge it up."

"But it's always there, always around us."

"It wouldn't be if you'd let it go. Just like this. You bring home that damn picture and go snooping around and she's back in our life."

I was hurt that he was mad at me for doing something any normal kid would do if they saw a picture of their mother. They'd want to find out more. "Don't get mad at me, Dad. I'm just curious. If you told me more maybe I wouldn't have to ask other people."

"But you don't ask me much about her."

"Because when I have in the past you get mad, just like you are now. So I'm afraid."

There was silence and then he said, "Well, what did you find out?" he asked.

I told him some of what I found out but I didn't say anything about the carnival man she was with. I figured that would hurt him too much. That night we made supper together. Dad buttered the bread for the grilled cheese and I put the cheese in. We both took turns turning the sandwiches in the fry pan. I studied my dad, wondering if my mom came back would she be interested in him. His stomach was beginning to hang over his belt and he was starting to get that full look that older men get. His tee shirts didn't sag with extra fabric. I guess he ate too many bowls of ice cream at night and cookies during the day. Usually you would think a kid would buy cookies, but when we go to the store it's Dad who loads up on Oreos and Snowballs. Dad used to drink more but lately he's been cutting down. He always has beer in the fridge but he doesn't seem to be drinking whiskey as much.

When I was in bed reading that night, he stopped at my door and knocked. He seemed embarrassed to come in. "Why do you close your door? You never used to."

"Because I'm bigger now and I like to be alone."

"Oh," he said. That was it. He stood there like he wanted to say more but it wouldn't come out of him.

"Dad, are you worried about me leaving or something?"

He looked startled. "Judas priest, you aren't thinking of it, are you?"

"No, but I just wondered."

"You sure?"

"I'm sure, Dad."

He looked like he was going to cry or something. "You'd better not even think about it, you hear me?"

"Dad, I won't." And I made a disgusted sound in my throat and turned to switch off the lamp. "I'm tired. Got to go to sleep."

He walked over to the bed and clumsily pulled up the quilt I kept at the bottom. I almost said something about it being plenty warm on this April night but I shut up. I figured it took a lot out of him to do this simple thing.

When I went to sleep, I knew that I wasn't done with my project. I was going to find Bea and talk to her.

A week later I was in the library on a Saturday and I saw her in the kid's section putting picture books away. She was kneeling, shelving *Madeline's Rescue*, a favorite book of mine. I used to like Madeline and think we had a lot in common. She was sent to a boarding school and she seemed like she was an only child also—like maybe her parents wanted her out of their hair.

I walked up to her and stood there a second before deciding what to say. I pulled out the photo that I kept in my backpack all the time, just in case. I held it up and said, "Recognize this?"

She seemed startled. "Oh my, didn't see you there." She looked up at me and then I knelt down.

"Weren't you in the kitchen band?" I asked.

"Sure I was."

I held out the photo and motioned for her to take it. She did. I saw her grin as she looked at it.

"That's me with my washboard and wooden clothes pin. But my hat wasn't much. Just a basket upside down with some plastic spoons poking up. Oh, I added that copper Chore Girl."

"What's a Chore Girl?" I asked.

"A pot scrubber—you know, the kind with copper wire strands that are curled."

I pointed to the photo. "How did you get that spoon to stick up?"

"I put it through the slot in the weave of the basket and taped it with duct tape underneath. See the ribbon? I had to add that black ribbon to keep it on my head."

"Yah, I see."

"Look at Greta with that other basket on her head. Hers was better than mine. See how she put the inside of a round angel food cake pan on top of her basket? Then she hung measuring cups from it. But it made a heck of a racket when she walked."

"Did you know my mom?"

"Oh sure. I mean I didn't know her well, just a little. You know she was so young and we were old cusses."

"Gladys said you saw her in Florida."

"She told you that, hey. Did she say anything else?"

"Nope, just that you saw her. When was it?"

"Oh, just two years ago. It was when Larry was still alive and we were snowbirds for the winter. I don't go anymore. I don't like going alone."

"Where did you see her and what did she look like?"

She was acting uncomfortable. And she turned on her knees and looked me in the eye. "We were visiting Key West. And I saw her coming out of a shop. She was tan and thinner, almost too thin. I called out her name and she stopped. When I went up to her, she seemed glad to see me but she didn't want to talk much. She just said she lived in Florida and was visiting a friend."

"Did she ask about me?"

Bea's smile disappeared. "No, she didn't. But we only talked for a second. She was in a hurry."

"Oh," my voice dropped.

"I'm sure she would have if we had had more time."

"How did she really look? Was her hair still long?"

"Yes, it was, but it seemed blonder, had more blonde streaks through it."

"What was she wearing?"

"I know she had shorts on because I remember thinking that her legs looked long and skinny. And she had some sleeveless top because I saw a tattoo on her bicep." Bea pointed to her own bicep to indicate where it was.

"What was the tattoo?"

"I don't remember."

"Was she alone?"

Bea paused for a second. "I think … well I guess she was with someone else. As I said, she was in a hurry. Maybe they were in another shop."

"So you didn't see who she was with?"

"It was crowded. There were a lot of people about." Bea seemed flustered and pulled her eyes away and shelved another book.

"Did she look like … she missed me?" I asked.

Bea paused. "I don't know. I suppose she might have."

"Was she with a man?"

"I can't remember. There were tourists all over the place."

"But couldn't you tell if she was with someone?"

At that Bea stood up and looked at her watch. "I have to get this work done. I'm sorry I can't be of any help. But your dad loves you and he's doing a good job of taking care of you. Just be grateful for that."

But I didn't feel grateful right then. I wanted to know about my mom and no one was helping me much.

I left the library and walked to the grocery store to get some things for Dad. But on the way across the street, I thought of something I could have asked Bea. I could have asked her if Mom had glasses or not. People who get older wear glasses and maybe Mom had them. I turned around in the middle of the street and went back in the library. I didn't see Bea anywhere but I knew there was a back room where the librarian had a desk and a coffeepot. I started walking back there when I heard Bea's voice.

"What would I say? Your mom has a little girl with darker skin like she's part Mexican or Italian. How could I tell her that? She asked me if her mom looked like she missed her. Gosh, I didn't know what to say."

I stood there not able to move. Another little girl. I had a sister. My mom had replaced me with someone else. That's why I never got anything from her for Christmas or my birthday. I bet she doesn't even remember my birthday.

And I hated that sister of mine. I hated her for taking my mom from me and I wanted to run across the street to Dad and tell him this news.

But I couldn't move. I couldn't even pretend to be quiet and sneaky. I turned and walked toward the door, bumping into a cart of books and knocking a few off.

Then I heard her voice. "Brigid, are you okay?"

I didn't say anything but kept going.

"Were you listening?"

I nodded.

"Oh my," Bea gasped. "What have I done?"

And I wanted to cry out: you've done it all right. I know now. And I will never be the same again.

When I was outside, I looked back. Bea was standing there with her hands to her face. And I didn't see my dad's pickup. I walked to the grocery store and looked around but nothing looked good. I wasn't hungry and I couldn't remember what I was supposed to buy. And what to do with this news? I wanted to tell Dad but then I knew how hurt he'd be. But I was hurting, too, and I didn't want to hurt alone. No, not alone. But then for the first time I knew I had someone like me—a sister who probably didn't even know about me.

When Dad drove up, I took a couple of breaths and walked out the door. I got in the pickup and was quiet for the ride home. A week later when the paper was due, Dad asked to read it. I handed him my paper and he said, "I thought you were writing about the kitchen band?"

"Decided not to do that anymore. I just couldn't get enough information."

Dad shook his head. "Good God, you went to a lot of work to find out stuff and then you didn't do it. I don't understand you."

I looked at my dad who was trying so hard and I felt I needed to protect him, to keep him in the dark about Mom and her other daughter. It would be my secret for a while, but I knew that someday I would look for them both and I'd find them. And for some reason I didn't quite feel so alone knowing I had a sister out there—someone who was probably lonely too.

The next time we went to town I took the kitchen band picture to the photo place and told them I wanted a copy. It would take two weeks. When I got it, I put it on my wall next to the dream catcher that was my mom's. Each night I look at Mom and wonder if my sister had been in her belly then or did it happen later. But I like to pretend my sister is there inside her and that this is the only picture I have of them both. And I think of Mom shaking her homemade tambourine to the sound of "Beer Barrel Polka," and it seems so out of place for her. But Mom was out of place here on the farm and in the kitchen cooking. Maybe Mom found her place down there in Florida with the alligators and fish and a new daughter. I just hope she looks at her daughter and remembers that other one she left behind.

the
Kitchen
band :part II

April 1963

*T*hey said she was back in town.

I heard it from two people on the bus that morning in April. Brandon Wise said his mother saw her getting gas at the Texaco last night. She had a fancy foreign car. After that, I heard Sharon Molloy say that her dad saw her and a girl get out of a car at the Suburban Motel.

All day at school I was fidgety. I had not expected my mother to ever come back. Since I found out last spring about my mom having another daughter, I expected that I'd have to go to Florida to find them some day.

During PE class I told the teacher that I had cramps, but I didn't. I just needed time to think about this, to figure out what I would say to her when I saw her. Would I tell her how angry I was at her for leaving? Was she coming back just to visit us? I hadn't told Dad that Mom had another girl but now he'd know.

After school on my way to the bus, I saw Dad's pickup. He waved for me to come over. I knew that he knew. Dad only picked me up if I had a doctor's appointment or was sick.

"Get in," he said. His voice was gruff.

"Why are you here, Dad?"

"There's someone we're going to see."

"Who?" I asked, waiting for the answer I knew I'd get.

"You'll see."

We drove in silence to the Suburban Motel. Dad pulled up in front of Room 10 with a black BMW in front of it. The plates were from Florida.

"It's her, isn't it?" I asked.

"Yup," he said, jittery as a baby rabbit. I felt bad for my dad.

"Did she call you today?"

"This morning. She showed up at our place. Just got out of the car and walked into the house like she never left it. Said she wanted to see you."

"What'd she look like?"

"You'll see. But there's something else," Dad paused.

"I know, Dad. There's another girl. My sister."

Dad spun his head to look at me. "How did you know?"

"I've known since last year when I was checking up on the kitchen band. I found out then but I didn't want to hurt you."

He sort of smiled. "That's big of you. But what's with keeping secrets from your dad?"

I felt bad. He seemed hurt. "I just didn't want you to worry, Dad."

"Isn't that my job?" he asked.

"I don't know. I guess it can be my job, too. I don't tell you when Buster gets into your stuff in the machine shed because I know it will make you mad. So I just clean it up." Buster liked to pull the tarps out and pull them around with his teeth. He also liked to get in the buckets of nails and screws and dig his nose into them and spill them.

He turned off the pickup. "Are you ready?"

I hesitated. "I'm scared. What if she won't like me?"

"Hey, it doesn't matter. I like you."

But it did matter and I wished I'd worn a different tee shirt and that my hair looked better. It was just pulled back in a ponytail. Why hadn't I worn it long today?

"Why can't she come out to the house? I think that would be … "

But before I could say anything more, she stepped out of Room 10. She was smaller than I thought she'd be. She was thin and wiry and tired looking. She had a tee shirt tucked into blue jeans. Her blonde hair wasn't so pretty. She had black roots, almost three inches, and the rest of her hair was yellow. It hung to the middle of her back. She was smoking a cigarette and she looked nervous, too. I saw her lean into the door of the room to talk to someone, but no one came out.

I looked at Dad and he was gripping the steering wheel and biting his lip. I got out of the pickup and stood by the door.

She came forward, dropping her cigarette on the sidewalk. "Brigid," she said.

I whispered, "Mom." It felt so odd to say that word. What does one do when they see their mom after so many years?

She put out her hand and I put out mine. We shook hands. It felt so uncomfortable that I wanted to turn around and run away. I didn't want to be here anymore.

"Hello," she said nervously, her eyes filled up with tears. I noticed one of her teeth was whiter than all the others like it was a fake tooth. She had a lot more wrinkles than I expected.

I looked down at her hand and it felt warm but rough. There was a diamond on one hand and I felt instant anger. How could she have a big diamond and a fancy car and never send me a birthday card?

I pulled my hand away and she looked hurt.

"I know. You don't know me anymore. I might as well be a stranger."

"You are a stranger," I said.

She looked hurt and I was glad. At that I saw a girl standing in the doorway, looking at me. "Mom," she said.

I hated hearing her say mom. Why should she be able to say it like it fit?

"Come here, sweetie. I'd like you to meet your sister."

The girl was only an inch or more shorter than me with brown eyes and brown long hair, and bangs that hung in her eyes. She walked over to her mom and said, "Half sister. She's not my full sister."

At that I turned to run, but my mom reached out and grabbed my hand again and pulled me back.

"You are sisters," she said firmly. "Brigid, this is Justine."

We looked at each other while she gave Justine a warning look.

"Say something," she whispered to Justine.

"I don't feel like it. I didn't want to come here in the first place."

I saw my mom twist Justine's hand. "She's tired," she explained to me. "We drove for two full days to get here."

"How come she isn't in school?" I asked, pulling back.

"I took her out for the week," Mom said. "I felt it was important she come to meet you."

I burst out, "Now it's important? What about all those other years? You never wrote or called. I bet you don't even know when my birthday is."

Mom's eyes filled with tears. "June twelfth." Her voice was shaking. "I do remember. I understand why you hate me. But I'm here to make amends. I wasn't right for a long time. I was drinking too much but I quit now."

I saw Justine lower her eyes like she was embarrassed.

"What's this amends stuff?" I asked.

"It's alcoholic talk for saying she's sorry," Justine said.

"Yes, it means I'm saying I'm sorry. I'm making amends." Mom looked up at me with red eyes. I was glad she was crying. She should cry for years about what she did. Her arms came around my shoulders and it felt odd, but good.

I didn't know my dad was even out of the pickup but he said loudly, "Amends. You think you can come waltzing back here after all these years and make it all right. God, I've heard everything."

Dad grabbed my arm and pulled me away from her.

"I know, I know I'm to blame." Mom took a deep breath and motioned like she was a coach calling time out. "Wait. This isn't working out right. Let's change how this meeting's going."

"There's nothing you can change, Lisa. You screwed things up years ago. Come on, Brigid, let's go."

And I felt Dad push me toward the pickup. He opened his door and told me to climb in his side. I knew he didn't want to have to walk past my mom again.

We got in and he started the engine and pulled out.

I looked back to see Mom standing alone with Justine leaning against the door of the room. I figured it might be the last I would see them. We rode in silence to our farm. It felt like a funeral. Why had she come back to stir us up?

I thought that was the last of her but she showed up an hour later with a bucket of broasted chicken, a quart of potato salad, and a tub of Dairy Queen ice cream. Justine was with her. Buster barked like crazy and wouldn't let them out of the car, so Dad and I had to go out and hold him back. I liked seeing Justine jump back, scared, when Buster jumped up and licked the window.

Mom rolled down her window and said, "I'm sorry. I did that all wrong. I bought chicken for dinner. Michael, can we sit and eat together?"

"Not with me, you don't," said Dad.

Mom didn't know what to do.

"I'm hungry, Dad. Couldn't they just come in for a little while?" I asked. For some reason I was glad they'd come back but I didn't want to show it.

"I don't want her darkening our doorstep again."

"Please, Dad. It will only be for a short time."

"Suit yourself, " Dad growled and walked into the house, slamming the door after him.

In a few seconds they were getting out of the car and coming inside. I thought for a minute of letting Buster go to see what Justine'd do but I held him back.

The three of us were sitting around our kitchen table ten minutes later. In that time I had cleared the mail off the table and I found a clean but wrinkled tablecloth and put it on. Mom found the dishes she'd gotten for a wedding present in the cupboard and set them around the table. Justine just stood there gawking like she was afraid to touch anything. Dad was in the living room watching the news.

We sat down together and I began grace. Usually I said the prayer real fast but tonight I slowed down. Justine didn't even know enough to bow her head and she acted like she'd never heard of grace.

"Where'd you learn that?" she asked.

"I've always known it," I said smartly. "Don't you say grace?"

"Nope. We usually eat in front of the TV."

Mom looked embarrassed. "We can say it if you want."

"I bet you don't even know it, Mom." Justine said.

Mom didn't answer but jumped up. "I need some salt."
She looked in the cupboard next to the sink but it wasn't there.

"It's above the stove," I said.

Justine and I watched her going to the cupboard. It gave us something to do. When she returned to her chair, she shook a lot of salt on her potato salad.

"Aren't you eating?" she asked Justine.

"I can't eat off a dirty plate." She pointed to a spot of last night's Hamburger Helper.

That did it. I jumped up and grabbed her plate and walked to the sink and washed it off. Then I took it back, dripping wet, and plunked it down the table.

"Thanks Brigid," Mom said. She gave me a smile that was just meant for me. And I didn't want to like it but I did.

"I'm not eating off this wet thing."

Mom soothed. "I'll just wipe it off. It's no big deal."

Mom took a napkin that came in the sack with the chicken and wiped off the plate. Justine saw that and turned away from the table, folding her arms on her chest.

Dad walked into the kitchen and grabbed two chicken legs and stood at the counter with his back to us while he ate.

"Justine, you need to eat," Mom said. "You've only had two candy bars all day. Come on," she begged.

Dad growled. "Leave her alone. If she's hungry, she'll eat."

"I just don't want her getting sick. She just got over the flu."

"It was food poisoning," Justine said. "The doctor said I ate something bad and I know it was that tuna salad you made me eat."

"I didn't make you eat it," Mom said under her breath.

"Did, too."

"Well, you're not dead," Dad said, "so it must not have been that bad."

Mom looked up relieved that Dad had come to her defense. I saw Dad look at her and she gave him a smile, but he didn't smile back.

I looked around that table and liked what it felt like. What if she stayed? We'd have this every night. And maybe Dad would sit and eat with us. I loved hearing this talk about flu and not eating right. Dad and I didn't talk much, just listened to the weather on the radio so he knew if he'd be in the field working the next day.

After ice cream, Mom said she needed to talk to Dad alone. Would I take Justine and show her my bedroom?

At first Justine sniffed like she smelled something bad in my room. Then she looked at my stuff on the wall and wondered why I had some stupid picture of women with pots and pans on their heads. I showed her Mom in the picture and she said she didn't believe that was really her.

"How old are you?" I asked.

"Eight and a half. My birthday's February tenth."

When I asked her what Mom was talking to Dad about she said, "Nothing good."

"What do you mean?"

"Visitation rights, that's what she wants. And a divorce. I can't believe she ever married that hick."

"He's a farmer," I said.

"He's a hick. His fingers are all dirty and he ate the chicken without washing them."

"They won't come clean. It's grease from fixing the baler."

"He's dirty, that's all I know."

She sat on my bed like she was afraid it would bite her.

"What about visitation?"

"Mom wants you to come live with us for a while, not all the time, just for vacation."

"What if I don't want to? My dad needs me."

Justine crossed her arms. "You won't be able to do a thing about it. The court decides."

I felt panic rise in me. I didn't want to be taken from my dad. I wanted a mom and sister but I didn't want to move or lose Dad.

"I don't get it. Why is mom coming back now?"

"Geez, you don't know anything for someone a lot older than me. She's a recovering drunk, you idiot. She's trying to reform."

I couldn't believe how she talked. She knew stuff I didn't know.

"So she doesn't drink anymore?"

"Not now. She used to drink a lot until social services took me away for a while."

"Why did they take you away?" I asked.

"'Cause she left me alone for a week. Didn't come home because she was with this guy getting loaded all the time."

"Where'd you stay?"

"In protective custody. It's where they keep you before you go to a foster home."

I sat on the bed with her. "Did you like that foster home?"

"Nope, I hated it. They made you follow all these rules and I had to share a bedroom with some retard."

"How long did you stay there?"

"Seven months. Mom had to go to treatment first and then stay in a halfway house for six months."

There was a knock on the door and Dad opened it. He didn't look good. "She's waiting in the car. Get moving."

Justine seemed afraid of him and jumped up and ran down the stairs.

The table was cleared off and the tablecloth was folded and hung on the back of a chair, but the dishes were still in the sink soaking. And now I'd have to put my hands in that greasy water and finish them.

Dad was mad; I could tell. Mom was in the car and Justine stopped before heading out the door. "You have to hold that dog.

I hate dogs." She was almost crying.

"He's in the garage," I said. "God, he won't hurt you."

She ran to the car and jumped in the front. Mom looked like she'd been crying and she had a cigarette pressed between her lips as she used both hands to turn the steering wheel and back up. She gunned the car when she left the lane and it sounded like she was glad to get away.

Dad just stood there at the kitchen window tapping his foot.

"Why'd she leave so fast?" I asked.

"'Cause she's crazy, that's why."

"What do you mean?"

Dad was twisting his hands together acting like he didn't know what to do with them. "She thinks she can come back here and demand visitation rights. God, I've heard everything."

"She wants me to spend time with her, is that it?"

"Judas priest, you're not going to, that's all there is to it."

"Justine told me she wants a divorce."

"Yah, and that's going to cost us money, too. And she thinks just because she's going to get married to some rich guy that she's reformed her life. He's probably a boozer just like she is."

I was stunned. "Getting married?"

"Yah, but she has to get divorced first. Maybe I won't give it to her. See what she does with that. 'Course it doesn't mean anything. She'll fuck anybody who buys her a drink."

"Dad!"

"Oh damn ... sorry." He hit the cupboard that was partly open with his fist but it just made it swing open more.

"She quit drinking," I said.

"Yah, let's see how long that lasts."

I felt my insides churning. Justine hadn't said anything about her getting married. So much for my happy-family-sitting-around-the-kitchen-table idea.

"I'm going to the shed," Dad said, heading out the door.

I figured he'd find that bottle of whiskey he kept there and have a few sips. That's what he did sometimes when he didn't want me to see him drinking.

I watched him tear across that yard looking like he would kick or hit anyone in his way. He scared me when he got this way. And I felt so alone watching this and wondering if my mom could take me away. I didn't want to leave my dad. He may not be perfect but he'd never forget about me for a week while he got drunk.

I went outside to sit on the back step with Buster. He liked being scratched and I hadn't done it for a while. It was cold for April and I needed a jacket, but I figured Buster could keep me warm. Sometimes I wished we would let Buster come inside but I knew we'd have a mess on our hands. He was always running through the mud and rousting out a skunk or coon.

I wondered how much longer Dad would be in the shed. If he didn't come in by nine I was going to go get him. It wasn't good for him to be out there alone.

The phone rang in the house and it went on five times before I got to it. I said hello and no one was there. I said it again before I heard her voice.

"She's in the shower," Justine whispered.

"So?"

"So I wanted to know if...," she paused.

"What?" I asked.

"Oh, nothing. Got to go."

I tried one more time. I softened my voice. "It's okay. What do you want?"

I heard her voice quiver like maybe she'd been crying. "Can I call you sometime?"

I wanted to be mean and say no way, but there was something in her voice that said she needed me. She needed an older sister to talk to sometime. "Yah, I guess so. Call anytime," I said.

"Okay, bye," she whispered.

"Wait. Will I see you again?"

"Nope. We're leaving as soon as Mom gets out of the shower."

"Oh," I said. "Hey, can you write?"

"Yah, I'm not a retard."

"Well, let's write, too. Give me your address right now." I grabbed a pen and an old spelling paper and I wrote down what she told me. But before she got to the zip code she whispered, "She's coming out. Bye." And I heard a click.

I hugged that address to me and knew I could find the zip at the post office. I could write letters to my sister and then she could write me. My sister. It felt good. I ran upstairs to my bedroom and looked at the kitchen band photo. Justine was right. It didn't even look like Mom. She looked a lot better than she did now. Justine had said she was eight and a half and her birthday was February tenth. So I counted backwards and figured out Mom had to have been pregnant when she left. So Justine was in the photo and didn't even know it. I had a picture of her—sort of. Then I took an envelope and wrote Justine's first name, but I didn't know her last. Was it the same as mine? It might be, since Mom never divorced. I wrote the address in big letters and studied it. I wished I had something that was Justine's. I'd ask for another picture when I'd write, that's what I'd do. And I'd send her one of me.

the rules of Fire prevention

Summer 1963

*T*he Connelly family lived in a fireproof house. Their first house burned down so they built a one-story house of block from the Block and Tile Company. Since they needed a new chicken house at the time, they hooked it right onto the kitchen. From the kitchen they went through an aluminum door to the chicken house and through another door to the outside.

But inside the house they had no doors. They hung a curtain made of metal chains over the bathroom door and the girls, Mardell and her sisters June and Lily, put a tall metal cabinet at the entrance to their bedroom so no one could see in.

I remember walking in the front door of the house into the living room with Janice and the other 4-H'ers and Mrs. Bauman, our leader, and feeling like I was in a new hog building. The walls were gray block with no paint. And the floors were cement with no rugs. They had four green metal lawn chairs and two long metal benches without backs. The coffee table was a yellow metal trunk, and on it was a mound of ruby-red glass. No pillows or cushions or throws were to be seen. A glass shade covered the light bulbs that hung from the ceiling in the living room. On one wall was a mirror with a silver frame and on the other walls were three copper roosters in various prancing poses.

I looked at my friend Janice and said, "Do you suppose everything's metal?"

They had no drapes or curtains on the windows. White metal Venetian blinds were in the living room and the rest of the windows were bare. And the windows were low so you could easily open them and step outside. There would be no drop to the ground.

Janice said she heard that they lost a baby in the fire so they wanted to make sure they had a fireproof house. We didn't see any newspapers or magazines or books anywhere. When Mardell, a freshman who was a year ahead of me in school, walked over to the bench we were sitting on, I asked, "Don't you guys read?"

"Of course, we're not dumb."

"Where do you keep the books?"

She answered smartly, "Guess."

Janice and I shrugged and then Janice had an idea. "In the bathtub."

"No, you idiot, they'd get wet."

I tried, "Outside."

"No, right here." She pulled the lid off a large copper tub and inside were newspapers and *Reader's Digests* and a fat book on myths and fairy tales.

"What kind of thing is that?"

"It's for holding water. They had it in the old days before we had water pumped inside the house," she said.

"Did it make it through the fire?"

"No, it would have melted. Everything melted. See that bowl over there?" And she pointed to the hunk of red glass on the metal trunk.

I said, "It must have been real hot."

"Real hot," said Mardell. "The house burned for two days."

Janice touched the bench we were sitting on. "So that's why you have stuff that can't burn."

"Yah, we don't want it to happen again."

"Do you have metal mattresses?"

"No, stupid."

At that Mrs. Bauman called us to attention. We said the opening 4-H pledge first and someone gave the treasurer's report before the program began.

"Today's talk is about fire prevention. And what better person to talk about it than Mardell Connelly."

Mardell stood up and pulled down her red dirndl skirt she'd made last summer for the fair. She smiled and walked over to the window with the blinds. I guess she thought that was the front of the room, so Janice and I had to turn around.

"To prevent fires you need to have fireproof houses. We have one. Look around you. We say, make your house so the fire won't have anything to burn. Then you can go to bed feeling relaxed. No fire can get you."

Janice whispered, "How can you relax on an aluminum mattress?"

We giggled and Mrs. Bauman gave us "the look."

Mardell showed us some posters she'd made that said that metal gets hot but it won't burn. They had two metal outside doors and metal doors on their closets so their clothes wouldn't burn.

"What about sheets and blankets?"

"What about them?" Mardell asked.

"They burn," I said smartly, and Janice grinned at me.

"Well, we can't sleep on metal."

"So you don't use blankets?" Janice said.

"No, we each have a comforter that we keep in the closet during the day."

"But at night fire could get that," I said.

"We have to be warm," Mardell said.

"I thought you guys liked the cold." Janice shivered and tucked her arms in front of her.

"Girls, girls," Mrs. Bauman jumped up. "Let Mardell finish her talk."

Mardell went on about some slogan called "Hit the Dirt and Roll." All I could imagine was someone burning up and then having to roll around on the gravel outside with fire scorching their skin. They'd have pieces of dirt and rock stuck in them forever.

While Mardell was talking, we saw a young girl peeking around the door. She stayed hidden most of the time, but I kept my eyes on her.

When it came time for lunch, we went to the kitchen to see the electric stove. They didn't want any flames around. When we were getting our lemonade, which was poured into metal tumblers, I saw the little girl again. I elbowed Janice and she looked, too. One side of the girl's face was deformed. She had scars on top of scars and it looked like her skin had just melted. When she saw us look at her, she turned and ran through the doorway leading to the chicken house.

After that meeting I went home and cleaned like a crazy woman. I took newspapers and old magazines that covered our coffee tables out to the burn barrel behind the machine shed and watched the flames jump and leap. I thought about that little girl and how she must have been afraid of the fire and what pain she must have been in when her face got burned. Back inside I took off the throw that was on the couch and that never stayed tucked in like it was supposed to. I took the three throw rugs from in front of Dad's La-Z-Boy, the couch, and another rocker, and carried them to the garage. I put our books from the library into a big crock we used for our winter hats and scarves. Then I swept the wood floor and wished I had some wax to make it shine.

When Dad came in that evening for dinner, he looked surprised. "It's so bare."

"That's to prevent a fire from moving too fast through our house."

"Fire, huh? Since when are you worried about fires?"

"Since this afternoon when we went to Mardell Connelly's house."

"I heard about that place. It's supposed to be ugly."

"It's real ugly inside and out."

"Did you see Clarence?"

"Nope," I said.

"Well, that's the guy you need to watch if you want to prevent fires." Dad said it like he knew something.

"What do you mean?"

"He likes to burn things."

"What things has he burned?"

"Remember the grass fire that got out of control last spring? He's always burning his ditches instead of mowing them. And some think he started that fire at the fair ground that burned the girls' demonstration building."

I remembered that because my sugar cookies never made it home last August. That had been the first time I'd ever taken stuff to a fair.

"Why would he do that?" I asked.

"He's one of those guys who loves to burn things. I've seen him at the tavern and he's always lighting matches and burning them in the ash tray."

"Did he burn his own house?"

"Some think he did. He had insurance on it."

"Then he killed his baby."

"Did a baby die?" Dad asked, opening the refrigerator and taking out a beer.

"Janice said one died."

"I think one got hurt but didn't die."

"Then that explains the girl I saw hanging around. She was burned."

Dad walked to his La-Z-Boy and sat down. He was mad that I'd taken his newspaper, and when he couldn't find his library book on ancient Greece, he got madder.

I stayed in 4-H for six more months, then quit. I wasn't the 4-H type. Dad was a little disappointed because he liked that I learned to bake cinnamon rolls, Tater Tot casserole, and sugar cookies. I didn't see Mardell at meetings, but I saw her at school. For some reason we ended up being lab partners in physical science class. It was taught by the high school chemistry teacher so he let us do experiments. Sometimes I think they were the same ones he did in his high school classes. Mardell didn't talk a lot because she always had some type of cold. She sniffled and blew her nose constantly.

Mardell was pretty dead-acting most of the time but when we got to use the Bunsen burner, she came alive. She loved lighting that thing. The day we burned the different chemicals to see what colors flared from each was the day her eyes glowed—her pupils dilated. She stood so close to the flames that Mr. Mathews warned her to stand back or he'd cancel the experiment. I began to suspect that maybe she was like her dad, so one day I got brave and asked her. "How did your little sister get burned?"

"You know," she answered.

"I only know she was in your house, but how did it happen?"

Mardell didn't want to talk about it but I kept pressing her. Finally she said, "She couldn't get the bedroom door open. Mom did."

"So that's why you don't have doors on your rooms."

"Yes." That's all she said.

I asked, "How did the fire get her face?"

"It got her whole left side. She wears long-sleeved shirts and pants so people can't see."

"But how did it just get her side? If she ran through it, wouldn't it be all around her?"

Mardell just looked at me for a couple of seconds, and then walked right out of that classroom. Mr. Mathews came back and asked what was wrong. I told him that she was sick.

The next day Mardell was back in third period physical science class where she handed me a newspaper article about using pigskin for grafting onto human skin.

"Did the doctors use pigskin on your sister?"

"Yes, on her legs and back."

"Does she have it on her still?"

"I don't know. She never lets me look at her."

Maybe that girl had power like Circe who turned Ulysses' guys into swine when they landed on her island. I thought of how I saw that little girl run into the chicken house that day I was at their house. Maybe she felt some connection with animals since she had pieces of pig on her.

Mardell continued to bring things about fire that she cut out of the newspaper. Sometimes it was an article on a huge fire in Chicago

that killed school kids and other times it was on people who'd been
burned in fires.

I decided to be nice and invite Mardell to my house on a Saturday
afternoon to help me bake sugar cookies. A few days before, I'd
bought a newly arrived pre-fall pumpkin cookie cutter when I was
in the hardware store with Dad. He was getting some caulking for
our windows, which scared me. What if I couldn't open the windows
and couldn't jump out if the house caught on fire? Dad said he was
more concerned about keeping the heat in the house than jumping
out of windows.

Mardell's mom drove her over to my house. I had cleaned the
kitchen and mopped the floor. She was quiet while we rolled out the
dough. When our first batch was done, I began making the frosting by
mixing red and yellow food coloring to make orange. Mardell put the
next batch into the oven but left the door open. The oven made
a hissing noise as the flames burned.

"You're letting all the heat out," I said.

She didn't say anything but just stood there watching.

"Do you miss having a gas stove?" I asked.

She nodded. "Sort of."

"I wouldn't think you'd love fire so much after what it did to you."

Mardell swung her head around. "The fire isn't to blame. It just
does what it does—it burns. It's people who start fires." She closed
the oven door and walked over to the rolled-out dough on the table.

"Like your dad?" I asked.

"He uses fire to help us. We burn our ditches like the pioneers did.
It's what happens when lightning strikes but we just help it along."

"But fire can get out of control too fast."

Mardell was having trouble getting the dough out of the cutter.
She reached into the cutter and dug it out with her fingers. It wasn't a
flat pumpkin but a mass of dough and she hit the mound with the side
of her fist to smash it down. "Don't you think I know that?"

I stepped back and watched her hit it again. "Hey, it's
just a cookie."

She seemed to not hear me.

"Mardell, we need to get the dough cold. That's why it's sticking to the cutter. Let's take a break and put the rest in the freezer."

She seemed to perk up. "I guess I sort of mushed this one, huh?"

"Yup, you did."

There was a slight turning up of the sides of her lips and I thought it was the beginning of a smile. She never smiled.

"Want some chips and pop while we wait?"

Mardell nodded. "Real chips?"

"Yup, real ones."

Mardell's eyes lit up. "We never buy them."

I was so glad that I'd made Dad buy them this morning when we went to the store to get our weekly groceries. We walked into the living room and I set the bag of chips and bottles of Coke on the coffee table that was cleared of newspapers. Dad wouldn't let me burn them so he found another Red Wing crock and he set it next to his La-Z-Boy. We kept the newspapers rolled up in that crock. Dad liked to read old newspapers and tear out stupid facts like the number of sturgeon in Lake Oahe, or that potatoes belong to the deadly nightshade family. He said the British probably wished the Irish would eat them raw because they'd kill us off in a sneaky way.

"Do you ever get pop?" I asked.

"Only when I buy it myself. Last summer I de-tasseled corn and I had money. I bought a six-pack."

"Did you drink them all yourself?"

"No, my little sister took two of them and wouldn't tell me where she hid them."

"Was that the burnt sister?" I asked.

"Yup. She's always taking stuff and hiding it. We don't know where she hides it but she's got some spot. We think it's in the chicken house."

"Does she hang out there?"

"She gets the eggs and sorts and cleans them. That's her job."

"Why does she sort them?"

"We can't sell cracked ones."

Mardell was eating the chips like there was no tomorrow.

She dug into that bag and pulled out handfuls. She made a pile right in front of her on the table. Then she'd take three at a time and stuff them in her mouth. For some reason I didn't even want to reach into that bag because it seemed like Mardell owned it. And her hands were wet with saliva from the way she was stuffing those chips into her mouth. Once she wiped her mouth on the sleeve of her sweatshirt.

The next weekend Mardell invited me to her house to make angel food cake. I'd wanted to learn how last winter so I could make Dad one for his birthday. Instead I made a devil's food from a mix and Dad said it was good but he didn't finish it all. Mardell said they made angel food cakes a lot because they had so many cracked eggs they had to use up. Then with the left-over yokes, they made a yellow pound cake with coconut frosting.

Dad drove slowly into the Connelly's lane, gawking around so he could get a good look at the block house.

Mardell and her other normal sister, June, met me at the door. Dad watched and yelled out, "I'll be by in three hours," like he was afraid to leave me there.

Mardell and June, a year younger, seemed happy to have company. I don't think they had many people over. June showed me three bottles of pop that were in the refrigerator. Mardell had run across the street yesterday after school to the gas station and had gotten them. The bus driver had been mad that she was late.

When I saw the burnt sister peeking around the corner, I asked her name. Mardell jumped in. "Her name's Celosia," she said.

I had never heard of that name.

Celosia stayed at the door watching us crack a dozen eggs into bowls—one for the whites and one for the yellows. I wondered if I'd be able to see the places where the pigskin had stuck on her. Would there be bristly hair on those pieces? The few hogs that we raised had hair that was tough and coarse.

After Mardell put the angel food and the yellow cake in the oven, she decided we'd bake another angel food cake so I could take one home with me.

"Cel," she called. "We need more eggs."

And at that Cel smiled and rushed to the door of the chicken house.

"I'll help her," I said and hurried after her.

"You don't need to do that. Stay here," Mardell said.

"I don't mind. I want to see your new chicken house."

I followed after Cel. The door was closing when I grabbed it. I was happy to see that there was a little room where she kept sacks of feed and oyster shells and a big crate of eggs that the egg man picked up. There was a screen door with an aluminum frame that kept the chickens out of the storage room. I was somehow relieved by this because I'd been thinking about the chicken house and wondering if the chickens ever got into their kitchen. What if this burnt girl opened the door and the chickens were waiting right there and slipped by her? Dad said chickens carried lice. What if they had lice in their house? But I didn't see Mardell itching too much. She just blew her nose a lot.

I stood in the storage room and watched Cel walk right over to the laying bins. On one wall were little compartments for each hen. It looked like a wall of bookshelves but broken into little squares. It seemed like there were a hundred squares. Straw was in the bottom of each square and the hens contentedly sat there looking out at Cel. They weren't afraid of her and she reached underneath one hen and talked softly to it. "Oh good, Esther, another one. That's two days in a row." She brought out an egg and put it in a metal basket. She went from one hen to the next, pulling eggs from only a few of them.

"Why don't they all have eggs?" I asked.

"I got them this morning. Some chickens only lay an egg a day and some every two days."

"Can I do that?" I asked from the screen door.

"If you want," she said.

I let the screen door bang behind me. The chickens didn't like the noise and a few jumped from their bins.

"Sh-h-h," she said.

On tiptoe I walked through the straw spread on the floor. I saw some chicken poop and tried to step around it.

I stood near her and watched her slip her hand underneath a hen. "There's one there," she said, pulling her hand away. She motioned for me to get it.

When my hand got close to the hen, she puffed up her feathers and her head jerked as she looked at me. She didn't want me there.

I felt strange, like I was doing something I shouldn't, when I slipped my hand under her. It was warm and then I felt something hard. It was the egg. I pulled it out. It was clean and toasty as if it had come out of the oven.

"She didn't peck me," I said.

"No, Sarah's nice."

"Do they all have names?"

She nodded, watching me with her beady eyes that looked a little like the chicken's. She didn't have any eyelashes or brows. I got a close look at her scars that were smooth and purplish in color. And then I looked at her neck and saw more scars. When she saw me studying her, she turned away and lowered her head. She walked to a lower bin and found another egg. I was mad at myself for getting caught.

When she'd gotten a couple dozen eggs, she walked back to the storage room and put the best ones in the crates. She kept ones that must have had some flaws even though I couldn't see what they were. Mardell was waiting for me at the door. She seemed peeved that I had followed Cel into the chicken house.

"Don't you have chickens?"

"No. Dad got rid of them when I was little. He said my mom hated those dirty things."

"They're not dirty. Cel cleans the nests and floor every few days. We have the cleanest chicken house in the state."

"Why does she name each one?"

"Because they're her friends."

"Doesn't she have other friends?" I asked.

"No, kids make fun of her. Chickens don't."

"Can't you do something to make her face smoother?"

"We can't afford it. She was in one of those hospitals for kids who get burned. We didn't have to pay for it."

Her mom came in the room and went to the chicken house door and called out, "Lily. Come here."

I said, "Cel's in there, not Lily."

She looked up at me and then over my head at Mardell. "I won't have this nonsense, Mardell. What did I tell you about calling her that?"

Mardell looked away and went over to the cupboard and slammed the door, which was open.

"You'll make that cake fall," her mom warned.

I didn't know what to do. June whispered to me, "Want to come into our bedroom?"

I went in with her and looked around their room. It was strange. Their walls were painted bright red. The three chenille single bedspreads were white, and metal shades on the windows were also white. On the floor was a painted rug of yellows, reds, and blues.

"Why does Mardell call her Cel?"

"She likes that name. I think it has some special meaning but she won't say what it is."

Finally Mardell came in and said the cakes were done.

We never did begin the other one, but Mardell sent home a dozen cracked eggs so I could make my own.

That week in physical science class our teacher Mr. Mathews was performing an experiment. He asked for a volunteer to be his assistant and Mardell raised her hand. He said he was going to show us what happened when Group 1A metals were mixed with water. He was going to add sodium.

I watched Mardell stand next to him with her protective goggles on. Mr. Mathews added the sodium and we heard some hissing and fizzing. He said if he added potassium it would burst into flames. He told all of us, including Mardell, to stand back.

He was only adding a little potassium because he didn't want to blow us sky-high. We watched with anticipation as he did this. Mardell, who was supposed to be standing back, kept inching forward like she was in a trance. When he added the potassium, there was a flame that burst forth from the water. Mardell asked, "Please, can we see that one more time?"

So he did it again. Mardell was only a foot away and she clapped when he had a larger flame that time.

The class was over and it was lunchtime. When I stood in line, Mardell wasn't behind me as she usually was. We were eating our favorite lunch—Sloppy Joes and chocolate cake—when we heard the explosion.

I didn't see Mardell after that. She spent the rest of the year at the Shriner Burn Hospital and then went to a group home for adolescent girls. Her face was worse than her sister's. Mr. Mathews said she was a person who loved fire—a pyromaniac. He should have guessed it by the way she loved to be near it and was always asking him questions about fire.

A month later I happened to be in the library working on a short story for English class. Our teacher told us to use the *Book of Names* for naming our characters. She said sometimes a character's name shapes them. I happened to run across the name Celosia on page thirty-five. It was Greek for flaming or burning. And I understood why Mardell had renamed Lily. And that week I heard from Dad, who heard from the men at the tavern, that Mardell had started the house fire and maybe she felt better now that she was burned just like Celosia. On page forty I found the name Ena, which meant "fiery one," and I thought of writing Mardell at her group home, just in case she was looking for a new name. Ena would be a good one.

hitting the Bull's-eye

November 17, 1963

I got up early to go to the bathroom because I felt a heaviness in my abdomen. I looked out the window right at the time when daylight began and saw three deer run through our yard. One doe had twin fawns that were about five months old—not grown yet. They ran alongside her as they crossed the yard and headed down the hill toward the river. When they jumped the barbed wire fence, they did it together like they had practiced this many times. Then running behind them, way back, I saw a stag with his rack of antlers. He stayed distant like he didn't want to be with his family.

I went back to sleep for another hour before getting up for morning mass. It was the third Sunday in November. Thanksgiving was coming up and we were having it with Dad's brother Elmer and his family. They lived up the road a couple of miles. I got tired of being the only girl whenever I went there. Sometimes Aunt Kathy was too nice, making me feel like an abandoned child. Aunt Kathy was having me over today to help make cranberry-orange relish that she'd refrigerate for ten days so all the flavors blended.

After eight o'clock mass, Dad and I stopped at Ted's grocery for chocolate chips and a newspaper. I felt like making cookies before I went over to Aunt Kathy's. I mixed up the dough and was baking my first batch when I felt wet on my underpants. I thought that maybe I'd dribbled a little. If I held my pee really long, then sometimes that happened. I ran upstairs to the bathroom. When I sat down on the toilet and pulled down my pants, I saw some reddish-brown streaks. For a second I thought that maybe I hadn't wiped myself good when I went to the bathroom earlier. But when I wiped, I saw pink on the toilet paper. For a second this didn't make sense; then it hit me. This was it. This was a period. I knew it was going to come someday and I was thirteen now. It was time. It was way past the time. Janice had gotten hers a year ago and she'd told me all about it.

I sat there for a few minutes trying to figure out what to do. I had to tell Dad since I needed some pads. I had one that Miss Hines handed out in health class for each of us to look at. I'd saved it and it was in my top drawer along with a belt with hooks at each side where you attached the ends of the pad. I rolled a wad of toilet paper and stuck it in my pants. I had to make it to my bedroom and didn't want to leak.

Once in my room I found the pad and belt and put them on. I was zipping my corduroys when I heard Dad call, "The cookies are burning."

I ran downstairs where Dad was at the oven pulling out the pan.

"Hey, you can't go wandering off. You could set the house on fire."

"I was in the bathroom."

Dad was digging underneath a cookie with a scraper. "We can still eat these."

"But they're burnt."

He wasn't very gentle with the cookies. A couple were broken. He put the empty sheet on the counter and went back to the living room to finish reading the *Des Moines Register.* We got one every Sunday and when we came home he sat in his chair for two or three hours and read it. Lately I had to find current events for school so I was reading and cutting out articles. Dad got mad if I cut out things before he'd read them.

I stood near the stove and felt the warmth from it. It felt good because I was cold. My stomach felt tender and I wanted to go to bed, but I had to get pads.

I walked into the living room. "Dad, I have something to tell you."

"Yah," he mumbled, not even looking up from his newspaper.

"I got my period."

I watched him. It must not have registered because he didn't respond. I said it again, "I got my period. You know, when blood comes out."

This time he heard. He stopped and lowered his newspaper. "You did, huh? When?"

"Just now. That's why the cookies burned. I was in the bathroom and I saw the blood."

He looked at me. "A lot?"

"No, not a lot. Just a smear of it. But it's going to get worse. That's what Janice says."

"Do you have the stuff you need?"

"No, we have to go back to town."

He let the paper drop on the floor and said, "Okay. Let's go. Ted's closes at noon, or should we go to Osgood?"

"No way." The Osgood store was small and there was no way to hide what I'd buy. It was going to be bad enough at Ted's, but at least an older woman worked the checkout and she didn't seem to ever look at our groceries because she moved so fast.

"Get your coat," Dad said.

He was already at the back door reaching for his keys, which he kept on a hook by the light switch. He had lost so many keys that I'd put three hooks in the wall for him to use.

I went to the bathroom and looked in the mirror while brushing my hair. I thought I looked older. And I wondered if people would notice, or would they just see the lump in my pants from the pad?

The horn honked and I ran downstairs and grabbed my coat. I stopped and turned off the oven and then ran outside. Dad was waiting, tapping his fingers on the steering wheel.

I didn't know what to say to him. Would he give me money and send me inside, or would he go inside with me? We drove in silence for a while, then he said, "Do you feel okay?"

"No. I feel a little sick."

"Maybe you should tell Aunt Kathy when you go over there this afternoon."

I glanced at him. "I don't want to go over there."

"You'll have to tell her. Give her a reason."

We had rounded the curve below the old Fogarty place. It had been a few years since they'd left. I wondered if Mary Kathleen had felt this way when she'd gotten her period. Just last month I'd learned from Janice that you didn't have a period when you were pregnant. That's how you could tell if you were "knocked up."

What would it feel like to have a baby growing inside me? Would I feel it move around and would I hear it cry inside?

"Does Janice have hers?" Dad asked.

"Yes, she got it a year ago. I'm the slow one. Do you know when Mom got hers?"

Dad shrugged. "Don't know that."

I wanted to call Mom and Justine and tell them.

When we arrived at Ted's, the parking lot was full. It was a busy place on Sunday morning since it was the only grocery open. Dad parked the pickup and took the key out. We walked in together. Once inside I looked around to make sure I didn't see anyone I knew. And sure enough a boy from my class was with his mother in line with six other people.

Dad seemed hesitant too. "Do you know where they are?" he asked.

"Yup, but I'm not going up there until he leaves," I whispered.

"Let's get a cart and get some things," Dad said. Dad pushed the cart and I walked alongside. He got a can of coffee and two packages of pink wafer cookies and I picked up oatmeal, syrup, and a cake mix because I like to make upside-down cake with blueberries on the bottom. That made me realize that I needed a can of blueberries so I turned around and went back to the canned goods. I felt my stomach hurting but couldn't feel the blood coming out. What if it wasn't the real thing? I thought it would flow out, because I'd heard girls talk about the flow, but I just felt sticky down there.

When I carried the can back to Dad, he was at the paper product section with his back to the big blue Modess box with the rose on it. He seemed to be studying the cleaning products. I looked around and then reached for the blue box. To cover it I grabbed a four-pack of toilet paper.

Right then that boy came walking toward us and I wanted to be invisible. He was headed right toward our cart and I couldn't do anything. The box stuck out like a cow with a crutch. The toilet paper sitting on top of it seemed to highlight it.

"Mom forgot the Kleenex," he mumbled as he stopped right at the cart and reached for a box.

He had the box in his hands when he turned around and bumped right into our cart. He looked down at it and I knew he saw the blue box because his face was red and I was red. Dad was off down the aisle pretending to study the cans of mixed nuts.

"Oops, sorry," he said, and hurried away.

I felt tears and turned away to wipe my face. Why me? Why did he see me? He'd go back and tell the other boys in my class and they'd all laugh at me on Monday.

At the checkout counter Dad and I didn't talk. We were the only ones there and we wanted to move fast. I wished now we hadn't gotten any other food so we could leave. The lady must have seen our red faces because she reached into the cart and took the blue box and put it in a large paper bag. It was almost hidden. Dad and I both perked up when we saw that it wasn't staring us in the face.

Then another bad thing happened. When she totaled the groceries, it was $21.18 and Dad only had a twenty. So I had to take the blueberries and a package of cookies back. I was so glad that we were up there alone.

But the lady was nice. "Happens all the time. I just did it myself last week. I had a ten and thought it was a twenty. Had to take back half my cart."

Dad never had enough money anyway and when this happened

I could see his shame, like he wasn't doing a good job of providing for me.

Once in the pickup, Dad gunned the engine and we roared out of there.

"It's okay, Dad."

"No, it's not. We should have been adding as we went along."

I didn't say anything. I could tell that it wouldn't do any good to talk to him. He would mope for a while then get over it.

At home I didn't put away the groceries. I took my blue box and went upstairs. I wanted to be alone. Inside the box was a booklet of instructions. It told me about how often to change and that I should take a bath everyday—that the blood wouldn't come flowing out into the tub. It talked about being extra clean and making sure my hair was washed, too And I should use deodorant and body talc when it was hot and sticky. I should, at all times, keep myself clean and looking nice.

I decided right then to go to the bathroom and take a bath. I would really scrub myself with Lux soap. I'd made Dad buy that brand for me two months ago because it smelled so nice. I hated that Ivory soap that he usually bought.

I locked the door today. I didn't want Dad coming in. Not that he did, but when I was younger he'd come in to check on me and wouldn't seem to care if I was naked. For the last three years I've been locking the door, but today I wanted it bolted and covered and a towel stuffed under it. I didn't even want Dad in the house.

I began filling the tub and got out a new bar of Lux. As I sat on the toilet, I breathed in the scent of the bar. It smelled like talcum powder and something soft and creamy. Maybe I should put a bar in my underwear drawer to keep things smelling nice. I looked at our bathroom and I wanted new wallpaper and a sink with a big mirror. This sink was stained with rust and the mirror was small and cracked. I had to stand on a stool to really look at myself long and hard.

I heard Dad's steps coming up the stairs and reached for a towel and pulled it in front of me. I heard him breathing hard as he stood outside the door. I didn't like it that I was sitting naked on the stool

with a thin towel held in front of me and he was two feet away outside
a sheet of wood. "Brigid, how much water are you running? Don't let
it flow over."

"I won't."

There was a pause. "Are you supposed to take a bath when you
have that thing?"

"Yah, it says to in the booklet."

"Well, turn that off before you use up all the hot water."

"Who else is going to use it?" I asked. Whenever he said that
I wondered why did it matter if I used it all. I was the only one who
took baths. Dad went to the basement where there was a spigot
hanging from a pipe and he showered underneath it.

"Don't be smart."

"Just go away. I want to take a bath in peace," I said. I waited until
I heard him go down the stairs, then I stood up from the toilet, letting
the towel slip off, and stepped over to the tub and turned it off.
When I looked down at the yellow linoleum, I saw two drips of blood.
I didn't want to wipe them with the towel so I stepped up to the toilet
paper holder and reached for a few squares. I wiped them and then
decided to get into the tub. I put my hand in it and it was too hot.
I turned on the cold and went back to my perch on the toilet. If I was
dripping, I should drip there.

I heard Dad on the stairs. "I thought you shut that water off."

"It was too hot. I'm adding cold."

I heard him going back down. Why couldn't he just leave
me alone?

When the water was fine, I got in the tub and lay there thinking
about me—a woman. I wondered what my mom felt. Then I thought
about calling Janice, but her family always ate dinner at noon at her
grandma's house and I couldn't call her until she got home.

I soaked for a long time and then I heard Dad's footsteps again.
"Have you drowned in there?" he said, rapping at the door.

"I'm fine. I'm getting clean."

"Well, I'm getting lunch ready so you'd better come out soon."

"But I don't feel like eating."

"You will this. It's a surprise."

I didn't want to eat. I wanted to be in my bed and to be with my thoughts. I got out of the tub and started wiping myself. When I wiped myself near that place, I saw a red stain on the towel. So a little did come out when you were bathing. That booklet wasn't telling the truth.

I used some talcum powder Aunt Kathy had given me for Christmas last year. I didn't know what to do with it at the time, but today it felt good to dust myself and put a little extra down there so I would smell good. I hoped the talc didn't turn sticky like flour does when it's damp. I attached each end of the pad to the little hooks on the belt. I wondered how long this belt would last. Would I need another one in a year, and where did I buy them? I'd have to ask Janice that one.

Dad called again and I went downstairs. Then I saw that Dad had made potato pancakes—my favorite. On the table he'd put two red placemats that we used for the Christmas season. He was jumping the gun on the holiday but I knew he was trying to make this important and nice.

When I sat down, he came over and poured me a cup of coffee. "I don't drink coffee."

"It seems that you've grown up today so I thought I'd let you give it try. You always wanted to drink it when you were little."

"Can I have some cream and sugar in it?"

Dad got the sugar bowl that we used for cereal and he went to the refrigerator and got the Half & Half. Dad used it in his coffee. I liked putting it on my cereal to make it richer and taste better.

I took a sip of coffee and it tasted sweet and bitter. But I liked the smell of it. I always had. Every morning when I smelled coffee while in bed, I knew Dad was up for the day.

We ate our breakfast in silence. I liked the pancakes but I didn't eat as many as Dad wanted me to.

"Do you want to help your Aunt Kathy?"

"Not really."

I got up and called Aunt Kathy, but she wasn't in the house. I told my cousin Ed Junior to have her call me back.

When I went to my room, I got my box of stationery and began the letter.

Dear Mom and Justine,

Well, it happened. I got it this morning. I thought it would be running out of me like it does when I go pee but it doesn't seem to work that way. I can't really tell when it comes out but I feel stickiness on the pad.

I'm trying to figure how to carry a pad to school. I don't have a purse and I only have my book bag. So how am I going to do this? I'll look stupid carrying a book bag to the bathroom at noon. The only other thing I thought of was wearing my green sweater that is long on me. It would cover my pockets in my corduroy pants. I could put a pad in the front pocket and no one would see it because of the sweater. In fact, maybe I could carry two pads—one in each pocket just in case I need both. I just don't have any flow like I hear some girls say they have. When does that start?

Wish you had a phone so I could call you. Write back as soon as you get this.

Your daughter and sister,

Brigid

Then I went downstairs to get a stamp before I sealed the envelope. Dad kept them in his checkbook, which always sat on top of the shoebox of bills in the cupboard by the sink.

When Dad saw me putting a stamp on the envelope, he said, "Who are you writing to?"

"Nobody."

"Come on. You're writing to somebody. Whose name is on the letter?"

I didn't want to tell him because he just got mad whenever he heard me mention Mom or Justine. Maybe he thought I wanted to go live with them.

He walked over and glanced at the letter. "Oh, them," he said.

"Yah, I thought they might like to know."

He shrugged and turned away. "Don't go expecting any answer back, or for her to send you some present. You'll just be disappointed."

"I got one from my half sister," I said defensively.

"But that was six months ago. They've probably moved by now."

"The post office will find them."

"Don't count on it."

"Dad, can't you just for once quit bugging me about them?" I kept the letter and ran up the stairs to my room. No matter what I did or said about Mom and Justine he always had some bad thing to add to it. Sometime I just wanted him to be quiet and let me alone with my thoughts about them.

A little later he came upstairs—this time with a bowl of ice cream with chocolate sauce on it. "I just don't like it when you keep dragging up old stuff. It's behind us."

"But Dad it's not. She's still my mother and I have a sister. I can't forget them."

"She forgets you." His words were sharp and hard.

"She doesn't. She knows I'm alive. And my sister cares. She wrote me."

"Suit yourself. You can tell yourself they matter if it makes you feel good, but I don't want you whining and crying in two weeks when you haven't heard from them. I don't trust that woman one bit. She's probably in California or Alaska by now. She doesn't stay in one place. And she knows where you live. And how many letters has she written you?"

I felt the tears come into my eyes. I knew he was right but I didn't want to admit it. I didn't want to hear what he was saying. I had never gotten a letter or card or even a postcard from her. My half sister wrote me one that I read over and over and even showed it to Janice.

I decided to do something that would help them along. I put inside the unsealed envelope another envelope with a stamp and my address on it. I even put in a sheet of paper so they couldn't say they didn't have any paper to write on.

All afternoon I lay in my bed with a pillow on my stomach because it felt good. I thought about blood and babies and

remembered Mary Kathleen's baby that was born dead and how her
brother hid the little body in a tanning barrel. I knew if I did it with
a boy I could get "PG." That's what they said at school. And I knew
about his sperm having to connect with the lady's egg but was it
always an instant connection? Was it like shooting a bow and arrow?
The arrow didn't always make it to the target's center. Last summer I
had gone with Janice to an Izaak Walton camp and they made us learn
archery. I wasn't very good at it. Most of the time my arrows went into
the bushes off to the side.

Dad came up and said my Aunt Kathy was coming by in a few
minutes to give me something.

"Did you tell her, Dad?" I asked.

"Yup, I did."

"Oh, no. She'll want to tell me all about it. And I know all there's
to know now. I read the booklet."

A few minutes later I heard Buster barking and a car stopped
by the back door. I waited and then I heard her voice. We weren't
all that close, not like some girls are with their aunts. They lived a
few miles away but we only saw each other when we had holiday
family gatherings.

I opened my door and watched for her head on the stairs. I saw
it. She was wearing a bandana over her hair like she'd been cleaning.
She had short hair and every Saturday she'd put her hair in wire rollers
in neat rows up and down her head. When she took them out, her
hair was soft and fluffy and you could see the roller marks for a while.
She'd backcomb her hair and spray it so it would stay that same shape
for a few days.

"Brigid," she called.

"I'm in here." She probably had never been in our upstairs. She
was always downstairs when she came. I hated to have her come
up here because our walls needed a coat of paint on them and the
linoleum was buckling and lumpy. One of these days we were going
to get carpeting.

She had a JC Penney's sack in her hands. She stopped at the door.
"So how are you doing?"

"Okay," I said, smoothing the chenille bedspread around me. It was a wedding present for my parents, and I took it because my dad didn't like it. It was a peach color. Dad had a quilt on his bed.

"Are you having cramps?" she asked.

"I don't know what cramps are supposed to feel like."

"Like you've got gas pains and they won't go away."

"I just feel sort of tender down there, that's what I feel," I said.

Kathy came in dressed in a pair of brown knit pants with Elmer's chambray work shirt on over the top. The red bandana was smashing down her hair and I saw a cobweb on it so she must have been cleaning.

"I got something for you. Bought it last summer at Crazy Days at the drug store. It's a starter kit for young girls. I thought of you when I saw it. And I figured I'd give it to you but forgot all about it until your Dad told me."

She pulled out a pink box that said "You're a woman now with a woman's troubles."

"Open it."

I lifted the lid.

Inside the box under cellophane were three different-sized pads and three tampons, a bottle of Midol, a new belt, and a small shaker of Johnson's baby powder. There was another book. This one was thicker.

I dug my fingers into the cellophane and broke it.

"Do you know about tampons?" she asked, pointing to the three in their neat little compartment in the box.

"I know about them but don't know how to get them inside me."

"Well, don't use them until you're married. Your opening's too small and you'll get them stuck."

I blushed. I didn't want her telling me this.

She pulled out the booklet. "Now you want to read this. It tells you all about stuff—you know, all about cramps and how long it lasts and the flow. Do you know about the flow?"

She sounded like my home ec teacher who would ask us if we knew about cream of tartar and what it did. "A little."

"Well, sometimes you get a lot coming out of you. The older I get the heavier it is. Lord, sometimes I have to wear a tampon and a pad and when I get home from church they're both full and I've stained my good skirt."

I didn't like how she whispered "stained" like it was something awful.

"Now do you have pads?"

"Yah, we went to the store this morning and I got that big box." I pointed to the corner of my dresser where I had put the box in a cranny between my little dresser with the mirror and my big bureau.

"Your dad went with you. Well, that's something else. Never heard of that."

"Of course, he had to go. I can't drive."

Aunt Kathy walked over and lifted up the big box. "This will last you awhile, but if you ever run out, you call me. I always buy two boxes at once. And I get mine at the Cotton Shop because they have them wrapped in brown paper and no one has to see you carrying them. I hate getting them at the grocery. They always stick out of the sack so the world knows you're "friend" is here." She paused. "You know what a "friend" is, don't' you?"

"I've heard it called that," I said.

She laughed. "My girlfriends and I thought we were being so smart calling it that. We didn't want the boys to know."

"Janice calls it George. She says George came last night."

Kathy came back and sat on the bed. "Now see those pills? Midol. They help when you have cramps. You want to take just two of them every four hours. Or sometimes I just take an Excedrin if I really feel crampy. But you know, I don't need them anymore. After I had my babies, I quit getting cramps. But when I was your age I had such bad ones that I had to stay home from school on my first day."

"They must have been pretty bad, huh?"

"You're darn right. And use a heating pad. Do you have one?"

"Nope."

"Well, now I know what to get you for Christmas. You'll need one. It just feels good to have it on your stomach. But make sure you put it over top your nightgown. You can get a burn if you put it next to your skin."

I saw the top of Dad's head through the railing on the stairs. He was listening and I wanted to say something but I didn't want to embarrass him.

"And this is baby powder," she said, pulling out the white container. "Geez, it feels so nice to shake it on yourself after a bath, and in the summer when it's hot and sticky, it makes you feel drier."

"I used the powder you gave me last year for Christmas."

"That's good. And be sure to change often in the summer because it can smell sort of like spoiled meat. Don't be stingy on the pads. You can always buy more. It's better to change them every three hours and not risk smelling. Men don't like that bad period smell. I read that some men can tell when a woman's having her period when they walk beside her. Some have good noses. So I tell myself that they aren't going to tell it on me. I take two baths a day—one in the morning and one in the afternoon, especially when I go to town. And I use perfume, too."

"I don't have any perfume."

"Well, the Avon lady was just around a few days ago. I'll send her your way."

"I'd like some Tabu or Chantilly. Maybe Dad can get me one of those for Christmas." I said it so he could hear. I saw his head disappear and I figured he moved to the bottom step or went down to write the name on a sheet of paper.

"And wrap your pads in newspaper real good and keep them in a special garbage can. And burn them every day. They attract rats. Elmer says rats smell them and Lord, you don't want rats getting in the house."

"Do they burn when they're wet with blood?" I was thinking of seeing Eleanor burning the bloody sheet after Mary Kathleen's baby came and it wouldn't burn. It was too wet.

"Yup, they do. The newspaper helps them burn. And don't go wrapping them in toilet paper. It's a waste of perfectly good toilet paper."

"Janice wraps hers in toilet paper. I saw them in the garbage in her bathroom."

Kathy rubbed her head like she had something itchy in it. "And she has brothers, doesn't she?"

"Yup, three."

"Well, she's pretty brave leaving those bundles for them to see and ask questions."

"Aren't boys supposed to know?"

"I don't want my boys bugging me and asking questions all the time. I like my privacy so I keep them in my wastebasket in my closet. And I burn them when they're at school."

"What about in summer?"

"I go out early in the morning when they're sleeping."

Aunt Kathy looked at her watch and stood up. "I have to get those cranberries ground up, so I have to run. Now, you call if you have any questions."

I couldn't believe how nice she was being. I felt like I'd achieved some higher status since I got this period thing. Aunt Kathy was treating me like I was her buddy.

"And get plenty of rest. I swear periods wear you out. Put your feet up and rest. And I put a towel on top of my bottom sheet when I'm flowing real hard. I don't like to stain it."

I nodded.

"Okay, now you call if you ever need any extra pads. And remember to burn your bundles."

Then she was gone. I heard her downstairs talking to Dad and I felt so cozy in my bed. I felt good with everyone worrying about me. I smelled cookies baking and I knew that Dad had put in another batch.

Soon I'd call Janice, but I just wanted to savor this moment for a while. I was a woman and I felt the connection to my mother and Aunt Kathy and other women. I had joined some club that only women belong to. I could now talk about cramps and flow and could give that secret whisper that I had to go to the bathroom and carry my purse with me. I didn't have a purse yet but I'd get one. And I'd seen that nod that even united enemies. I'd seen it with our teacher who let it be known that she always had pads hidden in her drawer in the coatroom. Last month Debbie, the worst student in class, had gone

to the bathroom and had come back rather quickly. I saw her whisper
to Mrs. Benson and they both went into the coatroom. Then Debbie
left and I guessed she had a pad somewhere on her—maybe hidden
underneath her sweater. Now I knew why I needed to wear a sweater
or vest. You had to have a hiding place for it if you didn't have a purse.

I longed to tell my mom and sister. If I knew their phone number,
I'd call them. I wanted to know when my mom had hers and how it
happened. I wanted to know every detail about it. No matter what
Dad said, I was connected to her and even though I wasn't running
alongside her like the fawns did this morning, I was a part of her.
I began somewhere back when she had a period, and then my dad
came into the picture. And that egg and sperm came together like
the arrow hitting the bull's-eye. Whomp. Contact. And I was formed.

the McGinty Girls of Osgood

Summer 1965

*E*very spring after the river found
its banks, we'd take a pickup load of junk to the dump at Osgood.
We'd clean out the shed and basement as best we could. I always
wondered how we could collect stuff when we didn't buy a lot. We
were always broke and just lived hand to mouth. Dad was the baler
and professional hired hand. That was a nice way of saying he was
too poor to farm so he helped out others.

With our pickup loaded with junk, we drove toward Osgood.
Once it had been a town of thirty people when the passenger train
stopped at the depot and dropped off and picked up folks. Now the
town had eight people. As we crossed Jack Creek, we could see two
tall elevators that housed grain bought from local farmers. The trains
stopped and picked up carloads of corn and soybeans and took them
to Chicago or to barges on the Mississippi.

Dad slowed down and turned north at the main gravel street.
Ten gray metal grain bins lined each side of the street. In the summer
Mr. McGinty, the manager of the elevator, kept the grass mowed
around them. Dad continued to the intersection. The depot sat right

there—a yellow peeling building that was empty. The sign *Osgood* was barely visible on the side of it. If we went east at the intersection, we had to cross the tracks. That's where the grocery store and gas pump were. In all, three houses were there on the south side of the street. A cornfield was on the north side. One house was connected to the store—the owners lived in back. Going past the store you entered the residential district—one trailer and a tarpaper shack. There was a deserted log cabin beside the shack that housed pigs and a few chickens.

But Dad and I didn't turn east. We went straight on north, slowing down at the elevator weigh station and office. Across the road was the best house in town. That's where the manager of the elevator lived with his two pretty daughters and his unmarried sister who wasn't so pretty. The house was a long bungalow painted white with green shutters and trim. And the yard was mowed neatly all the time. Peonies and lilacs bloomed in spring. In the heat of summer I could see a few yellow roses and some bright red poppies. There was a wire fence around the house and a metal gate that had a *No Trespassing* sign. A garage at the north end of the yard opened onto the gravel road. The manager had a new Chrysler that he kept hidden in there. Dad said it seemed a shame that he had such a nice new car when he didn't give the farmers hardly anything for their corn and beans.

When we drove past the garage, we came to the gravel pit area that looked like it had been bombed. It was full of craters and hills of gravel and crushed rock that the county crews used on the roads. There were seven different gravel pits in the area. The first one was the oldest and it was eerie—a shallow old thing that was overgrown with cottonwoods and covered in green algae in the summer. Further on down was the next gravel pit, our swimming pool. The county supervisor lived a half mile from Osgood and he had four kids who wanted to swim. So the supervisor used county money to fix up the biggest pit. His crew made a beach and brought in sand and gravel. They built a platform in the middle of the pit that had two diving boards. One was low and the other high. But you had to know how to swim to get out to the platform or paddle with an inner tube. This pit had cottonwoods and a few scrub pines around the north, west and south sides. The east side was the good side.

Dad and I went swimming only on real hot days when there was no breeze. Dad would blow up two inner tubes and we'd throw them in the back of the pickup and take off. Dad couldn't swim and neither could I. We tried to avoid people but many times the McGinty girls would be there sunbathing on their yellow chenille bedspread reading their movie magazines. Both were beautiful girls; one looked like Lana Turner and the other Elizabeth Taylor. Each had a white suit that showed the top of their breasts and they rubbed lotion on their bodies and lay down with their white-framed sunglasses on their eyes. They wore white headbands to keep the hair off their faces and yet they ratted and backcombed their hair so it puffed out around the headbands. And they had painted toe nails.

Young men came to the pit to see them. On a Sunday afternoon, the girls reclined on their blanket with their arms behind their heads—lounging and looking pretty. And the guys were busy showing off at the high diving board. Many tried to splash them. Once I saw Chubby Brennan do a cannonball that splashed them something fierce. They weren't too happy, since they got wet and had to wipe off their faces and sunglasses. They moved their bedspread back.

No one really sunbathed like they did. Farm wives came with kids and they stood at the edge of the water watching. Most people could not swim. Past the gravel pit were other pits but they were not meant for swimming. They were deep, ugly and dangerous with cold springs. A couple years ago a body of a hobo was found floating in one. All of the pits had bloodsuckers and you had to check for those black critters when you got out of the water.

The dump was past the fourth pit. This was the place where everyone dropped off their junk and where you found lots of good stuff. We'd see Erma from the grocery there all the time. She'd watch for trucks going that way and she'd take her wagon and walk toward the dump. She liked geraniums and was always looking for containers

to plant them in—old coffee pots and percolators—and lined them
up on the store porch. There were lots of blue and white enamel ones
and a few silver ones. Sometimes she'd find dolls with their heads or
arms missing and she'd pick those up and repair them. At Christmas
she sold them in the store after she'd cleaned them up and made
them new dresses. One year Dad got me one of them and I hated it.
I thought it was strange to see a girl's body with a baby head. Once
Dad and I were at the dump and we found a perfectly good picture
frame with only one crack near the upper right corner. A young man's
picture was in it and we figured the girl must have broken up with
him. At home I took out the picture and put in the photo of my
mom's kitchen band.

I never talked to the McGinty girls until that summer when
I got to work in the grocery store when Arnold broke his hip.
Dad happened to stop for a can of tuna and Erma asked Dad if I
could work for a while. She said she needed me as soon as I could
start because she wanted to go to Emmetsburg to the hospital to
see Arnold.

That afternoon I began working with only one lesson on how
to run the old cash register. Erma was a tiny lady, only four feet ten
inches at the most. I towered over her at five feet five inches. Dad
said I was growing like a weed and would pass him up if I continued
to grow like I had that year.

Erma showed me how to run the gas pump. I was to fill up cars,
too, and clean their windows. "But what if I have customers inside?
How can I do both?"

"You just take care of the ones inside and then you go out
there. People will see that you're busy. Besides, some folks fill their
own tanks."

A half hour later, in walks one of the McGinty girls.

"Where's Erma?" she asked.

"At the hospital."

She paused and looked me over. "Where'd she find you?"

I blushed and tried to take a deep breath and raise myself up.

"I live across the river on the river road."

"Oh, one of those," she said and moved toward the back of the store where there were a few magazines on a rack. She began leafing through them.

She did this for about fifteen minutes and then came back to the front without one.

"Tell Erma she'd better get some new ones. Those are as old as the hills. I have all of them."

I watched her lean over the ice cream counter and look down at the ice cream bars. She had on green shorts with a white sleeveless blouse and a pair of pink rubber flip-flops on her feet.

"How old are you?" she asked me, not looking at me.

"Fifteen," I said.

"Just a kid," she answered, opening the freezer door and reaching for an ice cream pie.

She held it, turned it over, and put it back down. Then she reached for a fudge bar and took that out. She fingered that and put that away. Finally she settled on an orange pushup and walked over to the counter. She took out fifteen cents from her pocket and dropped the money so I had to grab it before it rolled off on the floor.

I tried to look like I knew what I was doing when I rang it up. I was happy that the register worked and I didn't embarrass myself. I was hoping she'd leave but she hung around peeling the paper off the top of the pushup and handing it to me. "Put that there," she said, pointing to a wastebasket behind the counter.

I did it, feeling like I was her servant or something.

"Bet you didn't know I just won a beauty contest," she said nonchalantly.

"No, I didn't," I said.

"Don't you read the newspaper?"

"It depends on what one you're talking about."

"The *Emmetsburg Democrat*, that's the one."

She walked over to the front window and reached for a newspaper from the small stack of six or seven there. She held the newspaper in one hand and the pushup in the other and came back to the counter. She put it down on the counter and opened the paper, turning the pages, and then she pointed. "See that?" she asked.

I looked and saw her and her sister with crowns on their heads. The headline said, "Two queens in one family." Candy was the Palo Alto Fair Queen and Sharman was the Soil Conservation Queen. Candy had dark hair and Sharman had blonde. So this was Candy standing right in front of me.

I didn't know what to say so I mumbled, "You must be excited about that."

Candy glanced up at me. "We knew we'd win. One girl didn't even wear makeup," she said incredulously. "Poor dear, someone should teach her how to apply it."

I saw that she had makeup on right now. Mascara that made her eyelashes look extra long and thick and lipstick the color of raspberry sherbet.

"You must use a lot of mascara to get your lashes like that," I said.

She laughed. "Do you think mascara can do this?" She leaned over the counter and put her face into mine. "Look. These are false eyelashes."

"I didn't know."

She pulled back and rolled her eyes at me. "Do you really think you can win pageants with just a little mascara?"

With that she moved toward the door and shook her head like I was a real stupid person for not knowing about false eyelashes.

I was so happy to see her leave and hoped she was gone for the afternoon.

Next thing I knew her sister Sharman came in the door, wearing a pair of red pedal pushers with a pink blouse with the collar up and the top three buttons unbuttoned. She had on a pair of red plastic flip-flops. Her toenails were bright red but her lips were a pale pink frost. Her blonde hair was a lot puffier than Candy's hair. She had white sunglasses on.

She walked back to the magazines, too, and began leafing through them. Next she took a magazine and walked toward the front of the store and sat down on the window ledge and crossed her legs.

Then she said, "Got yourself a customer out there."

I hadn't heard anyone drive a car up. Outside at the pump was an old man filling a rusty gas can. "Who's that?"

"Nobody but Conrad," she said.

"Who's that?"

"The guy next door."

I watched as he filled the container and waited for him to come inside to pay but he just walked away toward the row of bushes.

I ran out the door. "Hey, sir, you didn't pay."

He didn't stop but kept going. "Sir, that costs money," I called out in a loud voice. "It's not free."

I felt my face get hot when I looked and saw Sharman laughing at me. I walked back into the store.

"He can't hear, you know," she said.

"He didn't pay."

"Oh, he always does that. He mows their backyard so they give him the gas for nothing."

I looked at her. "Why didn't you tell me?"

"You didn't ask. You just went skedaddling out there like you were Miss Store Supervisor. I don't know why Erma didn't ask me to work here. I'm taking bookkeeping and I know about running a business." She paused. "And I ain't no baby in diapers either."

I was getting mad and said, "Are you buying that magazine?"

She pulled her sunglasses down on her nose and looked up over the top of them at me. "What's it to you? I do this every afternoon."

The bread truck pulled up and I saw how Sharman leaned back more, putting her arms behind her and pushing out her chest. She crossed her legs, letting the one leg dangle and rock.

The bread man, in a blue shirt, waved at her and smiled before opening the back door of his truck.

When he came in with breads, cakes, and cookies on a wheeled cart, he smiled again at Sharman. "Got you those things you like," he said.

"Oh really. What things?"

He pulled a package of snowball cookies from the top of his cart and handed them to her. "Couldn't get the chocolate ones, just the white and pink."

She smiled and uncrossed her legs. "And what about the Heavenly Delights? Did you find them?"

"Nope, but I'm still looking. Maybe I'll bring those next week."

She reached out and took the package from him. "Thanks," she said.

He went to the first aisle where all the breads, cakes, and cookies were stored, and he began by loading up all the old goods in a crate. Sharman walked back there and stood and watched.

"Got any use for these?" he asked her.

"No, we won't eat old stuff."

"Well, maybe your mom would like some?" he asked.

"My mom's dead."

"Well, who's that lady that's with you all the time?"

"My aunt. She's our chaperone."

"I suppose she has to keep away all those young boys."

She smiled. "I don't care for the young ones."

He smiled and said, "You're something, Sharman, and so is that sister of yours."

He began putting new loaves of bread on the shelf and she moved closer to him.

"You know my mom was Miss Iowa when she was nineteen years old. That's what Candy and I are aiming for. In another year she'll run and in two years I'm going to."

"Really. Say, I cut out that clipping from the newspaper and I have it right here in my billfold." He patted his back pants pocket.

She leaned down so close that when he turned his head he was looking right into her blouse. "I sure do like those chocolate-covered grahams."

He laughed and handed them to her.

She stood up and walked back to her spot near the window. She opened the snowballs and ate one and then she opened the other package and ate another one.

All the while I watched this and saw how she got free food from this guy. I wished he would give me something but I wasn't pretty like Sharman. My sandy hair was long and straight and I pulled it back in a ponytail most of the time.

Right then I saw Candy walking next to the gas pump. She had changed her clothes and now she had a white sundress on with white high-heeled sandals. She was tan so she looked real good in that dress. Her hair was puffier this time. She didn't come in the store but waited by his truck. He handed Candy a chocolate cupcake and she smiled at him and touched his cheek with her hand. Sharman watched this and didn't seem too upset. He must do this all the time.

"Why's your sister all dressed up?" I asked.

"She's got a meeting with the Pork Producers." She left it there, like I should know what it was about.

"Why?"

"She's running for Pork Queen. The pageant's next week."

"How many contests do you guys enter?" I asked.

She stood up. "All of them. My dad wants us to win every pageant that's around."

I added. "Is that because he wants you to be like your mom?"

She paused and was quiet. "Something like that. He wants us to win so we get money so we can get out of here."

Candy stood on the porch and watched the truck leave and came into the store. "I need a roll of peppermint Life Savers," she said.

I turned to the candy behind the counter and handed it to her. "Five cents," I said.

"Put it on my bill."

"Erma didn't say anything about people charging," I said.

"Geez Louise, she lets us. We're in the store ten times a day. I'll bring it tomorrow."

At that, their dad's big Chrysler pulled up and he honked the horn. Candy started out the door when Sharman called out. "Why didn't you wear those silver hoops?"

Candy stopped. Her hand went to her ears. "I thought the white ones showed up more. Do you think I should go back to get them?"

Sharman shrugged. "Better not. The old man will raise a stink."

Candy turned back. "Tell me I look okay."

I was surprised by this. One minute she was acting so high and mighty and here she was whining that she needed her younger sister to tell her she looked okay.

Sharman walked over to her and said, "Don't fret about it. None of those hicks will even come close to having a dress like that." And she grabbed her sister's hand and squeezed it. There was a honk and Candy ran out and jumped in the car. Sharman followed and sat on the edge of the porch.

They were nice to each other. I felt a pang of jealousy. I wanted my sister to live with me so I could share with her. When I wrote Mom and my half sister last year after I got my period, I didn't hear from them for three months. Then I heard from Justine and she was back in a foster home and she didn't say anything about my letter. I knew that she hadn't seen it. So I wrote again and sent it to the foster home address. I got another short letter back. This time she said she didn't know how long she would be there because Mom had started drinking again and was refusing to go back to treatment. I felt sad and finally asked Dad one day. "Couldn't Justine live with us? The country might be a good place for her."

Dad stopped putting peanut butter on his toast and said, "What are you talking about?"

"I heard from Justine. She's back in a foster home and hates it."

"I would guess most kids would."

"Dad, could she live with us?"

"Are you serious?"

"Yup, I am."

He set down his toast and stood up. "The divorce was final last year. I'm through with that woman."

"But Dad, this doesn't have anything to do with Mom. This is Justine, and Mom's abandoned her again."

"I'm not taking up what she leaves behind. I always did that."

"So you didn't want me, is that what you're saying?"

"No, I didn't say that."

"Yes, you did."

Dad was sweating. "I meant that your mom was irresponsible and never took care of things."

"She took care of me when I was a baby."

"I took care of you more than she did. She worked at night and I gave you a bath and put you to bed. Most of the time she came home drunk and then passed out. The next morning she was worthless."

"I didn't know that."

"Of course you didn't. You were a baby. So I'm not surprised at all that she abandons another baby."

"Justine's not a baby. And she'd help me with my chores. And I'd help her with her homework and stuff. Dad, please, I want my sister here and this is the time to get her."

"No, she's not coming here and don't ask again." He threw his toast in the garbage and went out the door. I hated him right then. Here was our chance to bring Justine up here and he wouldn't even think about it. He didn't care if I was lonely most of the time.

The store was quiet. Sharman stayed outside, sitting on the porch with her legs dangling over the edge, until her aunt came around the corner carrying an empty clothesbasket.

"Come on. Two new loads of junk just got dropped off."

Sharman stood up and followed her.

I heard her saying, "You can't wear those things. I don't want you stepping on a nail and getting tetanus."

I thought about what she told the bread man about not eating old things and here she was, Miss Beauty Queen, traipsing to the dump.

There was always an urgent need to get to the dump before the county supervisor stopped by and started the stuff on fire. After it burned for a while, one of his crew would get into a bulldozer and push the junk further back into the fourth gravel pit. That was getting almost full and I wondered when they'd have to pick a new pit to fill.

I worked that day until Erma came back at five. She said Arnold would come home in ten days. So each afternoon when Erma went to town, I worked the store. And I had the McGinty girls as visitors each day. They must have figured I was someone new that they could pester.

On the second day, Candy came in but she didn't pay her five cents for the Lifesavers. She said she'd get it later. I had written a note with her name and what she owed. When I told Erma, she shook her head. "Don't let them start that. Last year I had to go to their dad to get the eleven dollars they owed us for candy. Arnold's such a softy that he lets them do that. He's taken in by their charm." And she let out a laugh that wasn't really a laugh but a snort.

Candy got a bottle of strawberry soda stored in an old refrigerator right next to the butcher counter. Arnold and Erma didn't butcher anymore and they just had hot dogs, bacon, and packaged sandwich meat in there. They had a few packages of hamburger in the freezer and that was it. No pork chops or steaks or chickens.

While Candy was drinking her pop, Sharman came inside, too. She said she felt like a Hersheys with almonds. Then both of them sat on the window ledge and watched me fill the candy bar display. Erma had told me I needed to keep the boxes full. She said they made lots of money off of kids stopping to get candy after swimming. And that day seemed to bring in a lot of kids in pickups who were headed to the gravel pit.

It was a sunny July day and I was surprised that Sharman and Candy weren't at the pit sunbathing.

When I asked, they looked at each other and giggled. "Our friend came last night." I must have looked like I didn't understand because Candy mouthed the word "period" and pointed to the boxes of Kotex near the toilet paper. I was mad at myself for acting so dumb.

"Why don't we ever see you over there swimming?" asked Candy.

"I can't swim and I don't have a very nice suit. I don't want anybody to see me."

Sharman added, "You mean the boys, don't you. You don't want the boys to see you."

I must have blushed because Candy smirked and said, "That's it, isn't it."

I didn't answer them and pretended I didn't hear. I kept my eyes on the Doublemint gum I was putting on the rack.

"What size are you?"

"I don't know."

"Don't you buy clothes?"

"Not many. Besides, I've grown since the last time I got some."

Candy and Sharman stood up and came around the counter to look at me. "I'd say she's a size eight."

I hated that they were looking me over and I just wanted them to leave but I was too chicken to say anything to them. I didn't think I wanted them mad at me.

"I have an orange suit that might fit you," Sharman said. "My aunt picked it up at last year's Crazy Days in Emmetsburg for a song. I wore it once but it wasn't for me. I look better in white. We both do. Shows off our tan."

Candy said, "We'll give it to you. It'll look good with your dishwater-blonde hair.

"Thanks, but no. I don't go swimming much."

"Oh, you would if you had a suit that looked good on you."

"You think so?" I asked. "Okay, bring it by."

At that a van pulled up and the guy who sold magazines came inside. I swept the floor as I watched him talk to the girls. He ended up giving them a couple free magazines that had ripped covers.

Sharman said something about wanting the fall issue of *Glamour*. It was wrapped in plastic. "Girls, I can't give you that one. It's a double issue."

After he left, I saw that Candy had one in her hands and was opening it up.

I walked over to them and said, "Where's your money?"

"Don't have it. Put it on our tab."

"Erma doesn't want you to do that," I said.

"Screw Erma," Candy said and turned her back to me. They both sat on the window ledge and read. They were so busy that they didn't see me counting exactly how many candy bars were in each box. I wanted to know when they took one.

It wasn't long before a carload of boys in swim trunks stopped by. They were happy to see the girls and begged them to go to the pit with them.

Candy said, "We're feeling a little under the weather."

With enough begging, the girls followed the boys out and got in the car and took off.

I was so happy they left the magazine. I brought it over to the counter and looked at the fashions that I knew I'd never own. I couldn't imagine buying these wool skirts with sweaters in pale pink and soft blue for school. What would the kids on the bus say if I got on wearing a new outfit with matching boots?

When Candy and Sharman came back two hours later, they were carrying an orange bathing suit and a shoebox.

"Here. Try this on," Candy said.

"Not now."

"Why not now? We'll watch the store."

"No. I'll take it home and try it on tonight."

"Come on," Sharman said.

"We promise that we'll watch things," said Candy.

I didn't trust that they would do that but I liked the idea that they had gone out of their way to get me the suit.

I went to the bathroom in back and as fast as I could I took off my clothes but kept on my underpants and tried the suit on.

"Okay," I called out.

They both came back. I stood by the door, nervous in the suit, wondering if they would make fun of me.

"You have to take off those granny underpants," Candy said. "Go back in."

So I went back in and took them off. I opened the door again and they were both standing there.

"That looks good on you. You have a cute body, if you wouldn't hide it under those shirts you wear."

"It seems too tight," I said.

"That's how a suit is supposed to fit."

"Can I pay you for it?"

"No, because we never wear it. It's not our color."

"Thanks," I said and went inside to take it off.

When I came out, there was a car at the gas pump and I hurried out but Sharman was already out there chatting with them while they pumped their own gas. I began cleaning their windows.

When they left, Sharman and Candy said they wanted to see what I'd look like with some makeup on my face. While I sat on the stool behind the counter, they put eyeliner and blush on me. I said I didn't want any blue eye shadow so Candy put some butterscotch-colored stuff on my lids.

I sat there so still as the girls worked on me. They chatted and laughed and seemed like they enjoyed what they were doing. They knew so much about colors and where to put stuff and how it would make my cheekbones sunken and my eyes bigger.

"We need to lighten up your hair a little. If you put lemon juice on it and sit in the sun, then it will get lighter. Why don't you try that?"

I enjoyed this attention. I remember a couple times that my mom brushed my hair and put it in pigtails. But she wasn't usually happy about doing it. She pulled my hair and I cried and then she got mad at me for crying. She called me a big baby and threw down the hairbrush and then she was gone. And I blamed myself. If I hadn't cried when she did my hair, then maybe she wouldn't have left.

This felt good. It felt like what sisters would do for me. I loved the attention.

"Now look and see what you think," Candy said, handing me a silver mirror with a long handle, like the kind you'd see on fancy dressing tables.

"Wait," said Sharman. "Let's take down her hair first so she can get the full effect."

I didn't want them pulling on my ponytail so I pulled the rubber band out of it.

"You shouldn't use that. It gives you split ends," Sharman said. "Use those big barrettes. Erma has some." She walked over to the shampoo shelf and found a package of three large barrettes in tortoise, silver, and gold, and brought them back. "Here. Use these."

Candy was brushing my hair and doing some backcombing. "You

have some curl in your hair. You should wear it down more."

"What if we trimmed a little off? It might not be so heavy."

"Yah, that's a good idea." And Sharman was reaching into the box for the hair scissors. Next they were cutting two inches off the bottom.

I was getting nervous because they were taking so long. No one had come yet and I was relieved.

"How about if we wash it and put rollers in it?"

"No," I said. "I'm supposed to be working."

"Okay, okay. Who put the bees in your bonnet?"

"Let's let her look now." Candy held up the mirror for me.

I felt foolish looking at this girl that I didn't recognize. She had too much eye makeup on and the lipstick made her lips look fat and swollen.

That evening when Dad picked me up at six, he squinted when I jumped in the car. "What happened to you?"

"The McGinty girls put makeup on me. What do you think?"

"I think I want my girl back. This one doesn't look right."

I felt hurt and angry. When I got home, I ran upstairs and looked in the mirror in the bathroom. I thought the black eyeliner was maybe too much. My eyes looked like those girls in India who put kohl around their eyes. My lips were too frosted with pale pink. And my hair was ratted too much.

The next morning at ten thirty I put lemon juice on my hair and lay in the sun for one hour. My hair got stickier as it got hotter. I didn't notice that my hair was any lighter. I showered before work and put on a white blouse with cut-off jeans and tennis shoes. But this time I let my hair stay down and resolved that I would buy myself some mascara the next time I went to town.

The McGinty girls didn't show up that afternoon and I found myself wishing they would come to break up the quiet. I had five customers and they all came within a half-hour's time. And then it was dull. I even wished the girls would have left the *Glamour* magazine. It was a long afternoon and I glanced at the movie magazines out of boredom and I read two articles in the *Saturday*

Evening Post. I had to be careful that I didn't finger the pages and have it look like I opened the magazines.

I went home feeling sad and lonely. I should have thanked them more for fixing me up. Maybe they didn't think I liked it.

The next day they showed up—both of them—with papers in their hands. They had spent yesterday in Spencer getting the applications for Miss Clay County Fair and Miss Beef Queen. Their dad didn't let them compete in the same contests.

"You're smart, ain't ya," Sharman said as she came in.

I shrugged.

"Do you get As in school?" Candy asked.

I nodded.

"Then you're smart. We need help. They want us to write an essay. Can you believe that?"

"Both of you?" I asked.

Sharman turned over her sheet. "Well, mine says to write three paragraphs on how beef has enriched our lives."

Candy jumped in. "Mine is worse. Mine says to write an essay of five paragraphs or more on why I want to become Miss Clay County Fair Queen. And it has to be typed. Do you type?"

"I took it this year. I'm slow but I can do it."

"Do you have a typewriter?" Candy asked.

"Yah. My dad got it for baling. One person couldn't pay him cash so he gave us a sort of new typewriter."

"That's great. You can type both of ours."

I wanted to question them about why I should do that, but I felt that somehow this was part of the agreement for the orange bathing suit and the makeup.

"Hey, your hair. It looks better down but you need some curl. We're going to get some rollers. They'll make a difference."

So they left me the forms with the directions and I thought about what I could write. I would ask my dad.

They returned with the shoebox and a coffee can with wire rollers. They set me on the stool. And Sharman got a glass of water and, with the comb, she wetted my hair for each roller. Soon I had a whole head of rollers and I hoped no one would come. But of course that's when I had a rush on people wanting bread and milk and hot dogs.

After two hours they felt my hair and decided it was dry.

"I just want some mascara. My dad didn't like that black stuff around my eyes and that frosted lipstick. He said it made me look sick."

Candy combed out the hair while Sharman put on mascara and blush and some raspberry gloss. I told them about using the lemon juice and Candy said that I needed to do it at least six times before I would see big results.

"Isn't there a quicker way?"

"Well, there is. We could use one of those Frost & Tip kits on your hair. You'll have to buy it in Emmetsburg and we'll do it," said Sharman.

"I think that would look good on you. You need something to perk up that hair of yours."

We agreed that they would do my hair at their house some morning in exchange for me writing their essays for their beauty pageants.

I went home that evening and asked Dad about how beef had made a difference in our lives. We talked about how it nourished us and how it gave us variety in our menus. That evening I began writing the essay. I wasn't very happy with it so I asked Dad to take me to Emmetsburg in the morning so I could go to library to get information on beef and get my Frost & Tip kit from the drug store. I said I'd pay him back after Erma paid me. He was a little skeptical about me buying a hair dye but I told him it was only going to add a few blonde streaks.

"You know those McGinty girls aren't the best influence. They may be pretty but their heads are empty."

"They're nicer than you think," I said.

"You be careful. I don't want you turning into someone like them."

"Dad, I could never be a beauty queen. I'm not pretty."

Dad took a sip of coffee at the table and said, "You're pretty in a different way."

I couldn't believe Dad was saying this. He never talked about how I looked. "How's that?" I asked.

"You have bright eyes and you look smart. I think that's a lot better then having fancy hair and glucking up your face with all that stuff."

"But I want to be pretty, Dad. I'd like to have people look at me and they never do."

Dad smirked. "You mean boys, don't you."

"I guess so."

"I don't want boys to look at you. I don't want them near you."

"Why?"

"Why? 'Cause I just don't."

"Well someday I might want to get married."

"That's a long way off. You're a baby still. And I want you to work on school and go to college."

"So you don't want me to be like Mom and get married at seventeen. Is that it?"

"That's right. And I don't want you needing attention from boys like she did."

"Was she pretty?"

He stood up and went over to the percolator. He got that at a garage sale in town last summer and it worked just fine. "She was pretty but it wasn't a good thing with her. She had too many boyfriends. Made her want to party too much."

"Did you meet her at a party?"

"No, I met her in school. We were in biology class."

"Did you like her right away?"

"I suppose. I should have been wiser but I was a young pup who hadn't dated at all. So when she paid attention to me, I was smitten."

"Smitten? Dad, no one uses that word."

"Well, that's what I use. And to this day I regret that I ever met her."

"But what about me? You wouldn't have had me." I felt so hurt when he said that.

"I wanted you. I just meant that she made my life miserable."

"When you say that I think you don't want me, that your life would have been better without me."

"No, I didn't mean that I didn't want you. I just wanted a wife who wanted to be married and I didn't get one."

"Well, if I get married I will want to and I won't abandon my children. I would never leave them like she did me and now Justine."

Dad didn't want to talk anymore. He washed out his cup in the sink and said we'd leave in fifteen minutes for town. He had to feed Buster and check on a part he needed for the baler.

On the drive to town, I looked at my dad. He wasn't a bad-looking guy if he'd fix up a little. He needed to lose some weight off his tummy and get a decent haircut. His hair was wavy and the longer it got, the messier it got. Usually he wore a cap and that kept it off his forehead. And he had a bushy moustache that I wished he'd trim sometimes. It hung over his lip and when he ate, food always got caught in it. I would have to remind him to cut it.

Once in town, we went to the library and I told the librarian what I needed. She found me some books and pamphlets in the file. She told me to go to the Extension Office for newer brochures. Then we stopped at the drugstore and I got a Frost & Tip kit and a tube of mascara.

The next morning the McGinty girls were waiting for me to arrive. Their aunt was vacuuming in the living room, which was real nice with a blue davenport with two blue brocade chairs and an end table with an ashtray and a picture book titled *The History of Miss America Pageants*.

They took me through their kitchen and into their bedroom. They shared a big room with twin beds. Everything was in pink and white. Pink painted walls. White fluffy sheer curtains. Pink bedspreads. Pink rugs on the wood floor. And they had a makeup table that I could have died for. It looked like what the movie stars would have in a dressing room. There was a big mirror surrounded by twenty or more little lights. It was long and two stools painted pink fit right into it. There was a pink-and-white striped skirt all around it. And the top had a glass covering. Underneath that glass sheet were pictures of movie stars and beauty queens. Along the back was a row

of tubes and bottles and jars. I had never seen so much makeup
in one place.

"Do you have it?" they asked.

I pulled the Frost & Tip box out of my bag.

"No, the essays. We have to mail them in tomorrow."

"Oh," I said, reaching into the bag for a large book. I didn't want
them wrinkled so I put them inside a book on antique tractors that
Dad had won at the opening of the new Farm and Home store.

They grabbed for them. "Oh, good. You typed them. They'll think
we're so smart," Sharman said.

Candy took her essay, which was the longest, and sat down and
read it. "Oh, I sound so good. This will get me into the finals, I'm sure."

Sharman said, "How do you know so much about beef? Gosh,
you're smarter than you look."

I didn't know what to say. I could have told them that I checked
out some books from the library about the uses of beef but I didn't
even bother. They didn't seem interested in what I had to go through
to get the essays done.

"Aunt Zeline," Sharman called. "We got the essays done. You can
mail that stuff in."

Zeline appeared at the door in her housedress with brown
oxfords on her feet. They didn't even introduce me to her but just
handed her the papers.

"They're done. We told you we'd get them finished."

Aunt Zeline didn't say anything but took them and looked at
them. She looked at me. "Did you write these?" she asked.

"Yes," I answered.

"It's nice to know someone can think straight and write it down.
Where did you learn how to do that?"

"I don't know. I just do my work at school and that's how I learned."

"I bet you pay attention at school and do all your homework,
don't you?"

I nodded.

"Not like some girls I know who dawdle all the time."

"Get going and mail those in," Candy said to her.

I was surprised they could talk that way to her. My dad would have slapped me for talking like that.

After that the girls got to work on my hair. They set me on one of the pink benches and put a plastic cap on me. They pulled all these little, long hairs through the holes in the caps. I looked like a porcupine. Then they put this stinky solution on the hairs and waited for an hour. They showed me their photo albums of the contests they had won already. It seems they had entered every fair queen contest for miles around. One year Candy would win and the next year Sharman would win. They had a whole row of sequined crowns on the tall bureau. I wanted to try one on but I couldn't put it over my gooped up hair.

I was so envious of them and that room that I could spit. My bedroom was so plain. Nothing fancy at all but the stuff I put on the walls. I wanted a dresser with a mirror and I wanted a sister. And I had one, if Dad would just let her live with us. I was determined that that could happen. Maybe I could invite her to spend a few weeks with us in August. Maybe that would be a plan. I would write her caseworker and ask if she could stay with us. Then I could work on Dad.

When the timer went off, they rushed me to the kitchen sink and had me put my head under the faucet. They rinsed off the white stuff that smelled like permanent wave solution. Then they pulled the plastic cap off and it hurt like the devil because my hair kept getting stuck.

When they washed my hair, I had both of them, one on each side of me, putting shampoo in my hair and rubbing my head. "You're supposed to massage the scalp with your fingertips. It stimulates the hair and keeps it healthy," said Sharman.

I didn't care what it did but I loved it. It felt so good with their fingers rubbing my head. I wanted this to go on forever.

When they put the toner and conditioner on my hair, they took me back to their room.

"I can't wait to see this," Candy said. "You're going to look like a different person with some color in that mousy hair of yours."

I saw blonde streaks when they tugged at my hair with a comb.

Their gentleness had disappeared. Next they put in jumbo wire rollers all over my head. They put a plastic hair-dryer cap over me and turned on the heat. It was hot outside and when I was under that dryer I was sweating like the dry-cleaning man.

I felt deserted when they left me in the bedroom with the dryer going but I had a stack of magazines to read. They had every movie and fashion magazine that was printed. I looked at the stack and wondered how many had been stolen or given to them by the salesman. If Erma only knew, she'd raise the roof.

When my hair was dry, they wouldn't let me see it yet. They brushed through it and then began to backcomb it. "I don't want it real puffy," I said.

"We're just doing a little," Candy said.

I felt the tug of the comb as they ratted the hair. I watched them work and they seemed to be totally caught up in what they were doing. I was an experiment that they wanted to be successful. After the hair was smoothed over with the brush, they went to work on my face.

When they finished, they had me stand with my eyes closed in front of the their makeup mirror with the lights. On the count of three I could open my eyes.

I did and felt like crying.

"Don't you look great," Candy said.

"What a change," Sharman said.

I looked at this girl with the big hair with blonde streaks in it and I thought I was their sister. I looked like them. I knew I'd wipe off most of the makeup when I got to the store to work and I'd comb through the hair, too. I didn't want it like this.

"What do you think?" Candy said, all excited.

"I look different, don't I?" I said.

"Yup, and for the better. We probably should have added more blonde streaks but it's a start. Maybe we can add more in a month or so."

"Yah, it just needs a few more all over," Sharman said, walking around me and studying my hair.

I knew that I wasn't going to let that happen. This was it.

I couldn't spend any more money on this stuff and I knew my dad would be mad if he saw me like this.

"Thanks for all your work, but I have to get to the store right now. It's almost noon."

I grabbed my sack with the empty kit in it and a clean blouse that I brought along. I felt sticky and damp and would change when I got to the store. Arnold was coming home today so I probably wouldn't be working much longer.

I thanked the girls and walked out of their house with my bag in hand. I just hoped no one I knew was going by the store on their way to the dump. I didn't want to be mistaken for the McGinty girls.

When I walked in the store, I saw Erma waiting. "Good Lord, why did you let those girls get to you? I don't think your dad's going to be happy with how you look."

"I'll take it off and comb out my hair before he picks me up," I said.

"Well, I hope so. I don't need another one of those bubbleheads around here. I thought you were sensible."

I spent a miserable afternoon at the store. I couldn't take off my makeup or undo my hair just in case the girls came over. And they did. They stopped in three times each. But at four forty-five I ran back to the bathroom and took a paper towel and wiped my face but I didn't have time to do my hair before Erma walked in and told me this would be my last day. Arnold was coming home in the morning and she was getting him bright and early. She would watch the store and him.

Dad looked at me real funny when he saw my hair and said they must have forgotten to use the whole bottle of dye because I just had streaks where the stuff worked. I knew he was teasing. "Dad, that's how it's supposed to be."

When I began combing it out on the way home, he didn't say anything. I think he knew better.

My first afternoon home in two weeks seemed too quiet. Dad was off baling and I wanted to be in the store. It had felt more exciting than at home and I missed Candy and Sharman.

A few weeks later I saw in the newspaper that they both had won their contests. But in the winter something started to go wrong with their pageants when they started to get more complicated. It was months later at the Miss Shamrock pageant that Candy didn't even place because she didn't have a talent. That's what Erma told Dad when he stopped by the store. The winner had a beautiful voice and was going to college to major in music. The first runner-up played the piano and the second runner-up played her flute. Candy had memorized a poem but she forgot it halfway through.

And the same thing happened with Sharman at Miss Teen Iowa. She took a few tap-dance classes so she could do a number but she just couldn't compete with girls who had practiced their singing and dancing for years.

Once I invited the McGinty girls over to visit, and they drove their dad's big car. But it didn't feel right. They were lost because I only had one *Glamour* magazine and no movie magazines. They were surprised to see all the library books and wanted to know if I really got through them.

Candy seemed more interested than Sharman. "You know, I could check out books for free, couldn't I?" she asked.

"Sure," I said.

"Well, I might try reading one. I've been thinking about college in the fall."

The next fall Candy left for a community college in Cedar Rapids because she didn't have high-enough grades to get into any four-year colleges. And even with that college she was on probation until she could prove she could study and earn good grades.

When she came home at Christmas, I didn't know her. She had on jeans with braid trim on the bottom and a baggy top that looked like African fabric. And her hair was long and straight and she wore very little makeup.

I was surprised when she came over to see me one day during Christmas break. She was driving a beat-up Volkswagen. She told me to call her Candace instead of Candy because she wasn't a piece of food to be eaten and devoured.

"What's it like at college?" I asked her.

She smiled and said, "Different."

"Well, is it better than high school?"

She sat down on the kitchen chair and took one of the butter cookies that I'd set out on the plate. "No comparison to high school. I like talking about the war and draft dodging and stuff like that. I've walked in two marches protesting the war. Wore black armbands and carried candles. It was cool."

"When did you do this?"

"Just last month. I'm in this twentieth-century American history class and I'm learning so much about our government and how corrupt it is. My dad gets mad when I talk about this 'cause he fought in the Korean War."

"My dad wasn't in Korea because of his bad knee."

"My professor was in Vietnam right at the start. He's against it. Says we shouldn't be sticking our nose into South Vietnam's affairs. We're destroying their country."

I was surprised to see Candy so animated when talking about war.

"What happened to your beauty pageant stuff?" I asked.

She laughed. "God, I am so mad at him for pushing us to do that. I told him and Sharman that those contests are stupid and ridiculous."

"What does Sharman say about that?"

"Oh God, she's mad at me. But she's a mess herself," she said, biting into a cookie.

"How so?"

"She spends all her time entering contests she can't win because she doesn't have any talent. I told her to take voice lessons but she won't listen to me. My aunt agrees but she doesn't have much pull with Dad. He thinks he knows it all."

"I saw her the other day and she's real skinny. Is she sick?"

"She makes herself throw up all the time so she won't gain weight."

"You look thin, too," I said.

"That's because I don't have any money for food. I live in an apartment with three other girls and we're always broke. We live on Campbell's soup."

"Do you work?"

"Yes, in the library. I shelve books. I love it. I'm just mad at myself that I didn't read in high school. I wasted so much time."

"But you're making up for it now," I said, sounding like I was her mother.

"Where are you going to college?" she asked me.

"I'm thinking of University of Iowa or Minnesota but Dad wants me to go to a smaller place."

Her face lit up. "I'm going to U of I when I finish with Kirkwood. "

She stood up and walked into our living room. We had just fixed it up, painting it and getting new carpet and a new couch and chair. It was decent. I had ordered white sheers from Sears and they looked nice in there. We had a new bookshelf and it was filled.

"My aunt's going to the college in town," she said. "I think she'll leave once she finishes and once Sharman leaves in the fall. There's nothing for her here. Dad hasn't figured it out but I can see that she's getting ready."

"Is Sharman going to college?"

"No, she's going to beauty school in Sioux City. I told her it was a waste but she won't listen to me."

"She might be good at beauty school. She's been fixing hair for a long time."

"It's not good for her. She thinks she's so beautiful and this won't help her much. She'll become more self-centered."

I couldn't believe she was using words like self-centered. "Maybe she can help others look good."

"Dad's throwing away money on it. He won't listen to me, but then he was the one who made us sign up for all those pageants when he should have made us read or take piano lessons or something that would help us."

"Didn't he want you to be like your mom?"

"But her parents made her take piano lessons and she won contests because she could play so well. And she went to college on a scholarship. He was so stupid after she died. He got rid of the piano when he should have kept it for us and given us lessons."

"Maybe he was too sad. My dad threw a lot of my mom's stuff away—burned it—because he wanted to forget her."

"Yah, but my mom was a decent woman, your mom was a flooz."

"A flooz?" I asked.

"You know, she drank and messed around."

"Does everyone know that about my mom?" I asked, my voice was shaking. I was feeling shame about her and it seemed worse that everyone knew who she was.

Candy's face changed. "Sorry. I shouldn't have said that."

"Did you know about my mom?"

"No, I didn't know her. I just heard people talk about her."

"Where?"

"At the elevator office and the store."

"I hated her for leaving and I hated her for what she was. And she's still doing it. My half sister's in a foster home—has been for over a year—and Mom won't quit drinking."

"Maybe she can't, you know. I met some folks this year who can't quit smoking and snorting. They just can't."

"But she knows better. She's been to that place where they dry you out and they told her what she had to do and she just can't do it—not even for my sister or me." I was feeling sick with this conversation and I could tell that Candy was getting uncomfortable.

"She needs help, that's for sure. Maybe if you asked her real nice."

I laughed. "That's doesn't matter one way or another. My dad asked her many times before she left him and it didn't stop her."

"I'm sorry for mentioning it. I shouldn't have. Anyway, I have to go. I told my aunt that I'd go with her to get groceries in Emmetsburg."

I watched her walk out the door and get into her Volkswagen. It had certainly seen better days. I would never have guessed that she would change so much.

The next day I told Dad I needed some soup for dinner so I took the pickup over to Osgood. It was snowing lightly outside but the roads were okay. I would be getting my license in a few months and Dad had been teaching me to drive. He sometimes let me drive alone to Osgood. We usually didn't see a patrolman on gravel roads.

At the store I told Erma that Candy had stopped by to see me and I didn't recognize her. She said she was as floored too. She wondered what drug that girl was on to make her change so fast. She'd heard of that LSD stuff and wondered if Candy had taken it.

"I don't think she's for real," Erma said, "She's just putting on another costume—getting ready for a different pageant."

"I thought she seemed real. She was nicer than before," I said. "Maybe a little."

"She said she was going with her aunt to the grocery and that seemed like she was helping more."

"Don't talk to me about that. I don't like to hear that they are going to another store for groceries. They come over here complaining that I don't have something and then when I get it they have already been to Emmetsburg to get it."

I could tell I hit a sore spot with Erma.

"What about Sharman? What does she say?" I asked.

"Ask her yourself," Erma said, pointing out the window. Sharman was in a lightweight coat that was unbuttoned. No gloves or hat.

Sharman came inside breathing heavily. "Damn, it's cold out there."

"Well, dress right and you won't notice it so much," said Erma.

She nodded at me and said, "He let you drive over here? What's with him?"

"He was watching TV and didn't want to leave."

"Have you seen Candace?" Sharman asked, emphasizing the "ace" on her name

I nodded.

"Thinks she's so smart because she works in a library. I bet she doesn't read half the books she talks about."

"I think she read a few," I said.

"Yah sure, I see her bringing these books home in her backpack and I ain't seen her read too many yet this vacation. Then what does she give me for a present? Two stupid books and she gives my dad and aunt books. God, you'd think she was Miss Library or something."

"What'd she give you?" I asked, curious as to what she would select.

"Some book about on the road and another called *Howl*. As soon as she leaves I'm going throw them in the dump."

"No, don't. I'll take them." It would kill me to have her toss them.

"You know, I need you to write me an essay for Miss Shamrock. Can you get it done by next Tuesday?"

"What's it about?"

"Oh, something about the meaning of this Irish celebration. I figured you knew all about the Irish with your name Brigid. Walk over with me to the house and I'll give it to you."

I zipped up my coat, paid for the cream of mushroom soup and walked out the door following Sharman who was running ahead.

Five minutes later we closed the front door to her house, and I took off my coat and followed her to her bedroom. Candy was lying on the bed on her stomach reading a book. The bedroom had changed. Candy's side had new posters up with sayings about peace and love and stuff like that. She no longer had the pink chenille bedspread but an African-print cloth covering her bed. It looked more like a tablecloth. And I smelled incense and saw that on her nightstand she had a stick burning. It smelled good.

She nodded at me when I entered the room.

Sharman went to her dresser where she had a stack of papers. She pulled out an envelope and found the sheet of paper inside.

"Here it is. It needs to be five hundred words," she said to me.

Candy rolled over. "Why don't you do it yourself? If you're going to enter that stupid contest at least you can be honest about it. If they found out you were plagiarizing, you could be kicked out."

"Just keep your nose out of it," Sharman shot back.

Candy turned to me. "Why are you helping her cheat?"

I didn't know what to say. I felt ashamed standing there between the two of them. I wished now I hadn't come over there.

"And you won't win. I've been there. You need to have some real talent—not a stupid tap dance that a five-year-old could do."

At that Sharman burst into tears and ran out of the room calling for her dad. I followed after her, grabbed my coat from the hall tree and opened the front door.

I felt the cold wind rip through me as I ran back to the store to get the pickup. When I got to my pickup, Erma was motioning for me to come inside. I didn't want to but I knew I had to see what she wanted.

"Can you believe how those two carry on?" she said. "Each one's been over here complaining about the other one. Their aunt says she can't stand it. She might have Candy sleep on the couch so they don't fight so much."

I looked at Erma sitting on the stool behind the counter. She was dressed warm with a red sweatshirt with Christmas bells on the front and a heavy gray cardigan pulled over that.

"College has changed her a lot."

"There's nothing like a reformed whore," said Erma. "She acts like she's the brain of the campus. I think most of it's for show."

"I saw her reading," I said, coming to her defense.

"Yah, you saw it but how much was going into that brain of hers?"

"Candy said her aunt is taking classes at the local college." I wanted to change the subject.

"That's what I heard. I don't know why she's doing it at her age."

"She might move out and get a job."

"I don't believe that."

"That's what Candy said."

"Well, he took her in when she didn't have a pot to pee in and then she'll abandon him when all the girls are gone."

"Maybe she wants her own life," I said. "I don't think she seemed real happy."

"Happy. What's with this happy thing? You live and die and that's about it."

"I have to go home and make dinner." I didn't want to stand there and listen to Erma and I didn't want to run into Sharman again. I was bothered by what Candy said about plagiarizing and I didn't want to do that again either.

As I drove home in the pickup, the snow was coming down heavily. I knew Dad would be upset that I had taken so long. Three deer ran across the road in front of me and I slowed down even more. At dusk the deer were heading toward the river. But how could they drink with the ice covering it?

Dad was waiting at the door when I drove up. He'd been worrying, I could tell. I went to work making the casserole. I browned the hamburger with diced onion and put that into the bottom of the pan. Then I added green beans, soup, and Tater Tots on the top and put this in the oven at 375°.

For the next few days I kept waiting for Sharman to show up with the papers on the essay for Miss Shamrock but she didn't. I was glad I didn't run into her at school. We didn't have any classes together and I ate my lunch earlier than she did.

I tried not to think about the girls but they kept popping into my brain. Toward the end of January, Dad said he saw an ambulance going to Osgood. We could see the red lights from our view on the river bluff. We both thought that it must be Arnold—that he'd had a heart attack. But the next day at school I heard some kids whispering about Sharman trying to do herself in. She had slashed her wrists in the bathtub.

I felt very upset by this. Had I done it? Was I to blame for not filling out the essay for her? Had I abandoned her? All these things kept racing through my mind and I decided I had to stop at the hospital to see her. So after school I told Dad I was getting a ride to the hospital to visit Sharman. Could he pick me up there?

I saw Candy outside the room when I walked down the hall. She was happy to see me and came over and hugged me. This was something she didn't do.

"How'd she do it?" I asked.

"Took a piece of glass and just whacked away at her wrists. She did both of them."

"Glass?"

"Yah, a glass piece she picked up at the dump. She used her favorite red one."

"Her favorite. Does she have a lot?"

"She collects them. She has a cigar box full of pieces—some blue and yellow but her favorites were the red ones."

"Will she be okay?" I asked, looking in the room. She was sleeping in the bed and her aunt was sitting by the bed reading a book.

"She has to go away to a hospital."

"Why?" I asked.

"Because she's starving herself."

I looked closer and saw that she was thin but I thought she was just getting ready for a beauty contest. "Will she be able to enter Miss Shamrock?"

Candy laughed. "I hope not."

"Did she ever get the essay written?"

"No, she didn't get anything written, not even her name on the application. She just quit doing anything, including school. She's been home sick most of the month."

We talked for a bit more and then I left. On the way home with my dad I told him about Sharman and her not eating.

"Now, don't you go doing anything stupid like that," he said.

"I won't. I don't enter beauty pageants so I don't have to worry about how I look."

"Well, those girls didn't gain anything from going to all those contests. They're both messed up right now. One's on drugs and the other's starving herself."

"Candy's not on drugs," I said.

"Are you sure about that?"

"No, but she's reading more. She wouldn't mess up her brain with drugs, would she?"

"I can't answer that. I just heard Arnold and Erma say that they saw her smoking out by the dump one day. They said it smelled real sweet and she threw it down when they got near her. Erma picked it up and said it was a hand-rolled jobby."

"She never did like those girls. She'd make up anything to get them in trouble."

Dad turned his head and gave me a funny look. "I'm just relaying what she said. I'm not making it up."

I didn't say anything more. I was real confused about how I felt about the girls. On one hand I felt loyal toward them because they had been nice to me and had fixed me up. They had pampered me and taught me about trying to look nice. Yet they had been such showoffs that they made me mad a lot. I still thought of them as my McGinty girls. They made the town of Osgood seem exciting to me. They made the dump, the swimming pit, and the store come alive. I had never been bored when I worked in Erma's store and had them as visitors. And I felt a real sadness that they would be gone from the place soon.

But the worst thing that happened was a few weeks later. Erma had a heart attack and died. I saw the McGinty girls at the funeral, which was in Graettinger, not Emmetsburg. Erma had gone to the Methodist church there. Sharman was fragile and skinny; she walked like she was going to fall apart and they wouldn't be able to pick up the pieces. Candy, wearing a long dress in some foreign fabric, cried and cried. The aunt had a new dress on and had her hair cut short and frosted. She wore earrings. I didn't recognize her. She didn't look so mousy anymore. Dad said she had found an apartment in Emmetsburg and was working at Mary's Style Shop during the day and helping at the library three nights a week. And their dad just stood there staring straight ahead like things were normal.

Arnold couldn't keep up the store. He sold what groceries he had in there and closed it down. Some days Dad and I could see him sitting behind the counter of the empty store, just watching out the window. And the coffee pots of geraniums withered and died. He wasn't taking care of anything. There was some gas left in the pump and the old coot next door came and filled his gas can all the time and mowed his lawn.

Sharman went away right after that. She was in the crazy ward of a hospital and Candy went back to college. The aunt was living in town. And their dad was all alone. I told Dad that the town now had four men in it and no women.

When we went to the dump that summer, it seemed boring. I couldn't find anything worth keeping. I didn't even spot a colored piece of glass or a doll arm. It was just stinky paper diapers and cans and someone had dropped off a 1959 Ford. There was also an old wringer washing machine and the butcher counter from the store. I don't know how it got there. Arnold couldn't carry it.

At the end of summer, the county supervisor closed the dump because people were abusing it. They were dumping off stuff that wasn't good junk. And the rats were everywhere, especially eating the grain in the bins. When we went in September, there was a snow fence in front of the dump and a sign said *CLOSED*.

The McGinty girls didn't come home that Christmas. Candace had gotten in trouble for defacing public property with spray paint and was doing community service. Sharman was in a halfway house and struggling. The aunt was doing the best of anyone. She was the top saleswoman at Mary's Style Shop and had started a book club that met once a month on Wednesday nights at the library. Mr. McGinty moved to Fenton to run that elevator. Their house stood empty because the new elevator manager ran operations in both Graettinger and Osgood, and he lived in Graettinger.

Dad and I went swimming once that summer but the gravel pit was just a gravel pit. I saw it clearly then. There were no McGinty girls on the blanket for us to stare at. The bloodsuckers were more plentiful and I found two on me and said I'd never return. That summer Emmetsburg built a new swimming pool and folks were going there to swim and take lessons. The young men flocked to that area to watch the bathing beauties seated on bright beach towels. And I prepared for college and leaving my dad.

Horsey
people

1966

*T*hat fall when the ears of corn were ready to be picked, I remembered how the pollen from the male tassels got near the female ears and that made kernels. I thought, too, of soybeans with their dry pod bursting, just like a woman ready to spill out quintuplets.

And I wanted to get to know a guy, to talk to one. I was sixteen and hadn't had a real date and wondered if any decent guy would ever like me. Then Dusty O'Leary moved onto the Fogarty place and took a liking to me. The house on the Fogarty place wasn't fit for humans, since it had been left open for years, but it was okay for the chickens they kept in there. The O'Learys lived in a pink and white trailer. The mom worked in the egg factory in town. That's where they candled the eggs to see if they were fertile. If the eggs were okay, they packed them in crates and sent them to a place where they were sold to grocery stores. A few times she brought home eggs that were ready to hatch and that's how they got the chickens that were running in and out the front door of the old house. But mostly she brought home eggs that were cracked.

The dad wasn't around much. He was a trucker who came home every two weeks and parked his big rig at the end of the lane. There was a younger sister named Prudence that Dusty was supposed to babysit. She was twelve, and a burly girl.

Dusty, the oldest, was strange. Something was missing in him. In September he started coming down to see me on his horse named Tyrone, a feisty stallion. It was jittery and acted like it would bolt every time there was a noise. I didn't want to get close to it.

The first time Dusty rode into my lane, Buster barked like all get-out and I heard a loud whistle. When I poked my head out the back door, there was Dusty sitting on his horse, wearing a dirty-white tee shirt, jeans, and worn black cowboy boots. "Get this dog to shut up," he said. "It's scaring Tyrone."

"Buster can bark all he wants to," I said. "That's his job."

When he saw that I wasn't going to hold Buster and quiet him down, he left.

That evening at supper, I told Dad about Dusty coming by. "You stay away from him," said Dad. "He's one of those horsey people." And I knew what he meant. They were quirky and sort of queer, too, but not queer in the sex way. I didn't know another name for how they acted. But I remembered Adelaide and her retarded son who looked like a girl. They'd moved away a few years ago.

But Dusty was not to be stopped. He came again and again, racing into the lane on that stallion, coming right up to the back door and pulling on the reins for the horse to stop. And then he'd whistle or call out while peeking in the kitchen window.

Buster barked but Dusty quieted him by throwing him something to eat and that made me mad. I didn't think they had anything to eat at that house except eggs.

I came to the kitchen door and held it open, "Don't you be throwing bones to my dog," I said.

"It keeps him quiet so we can talk."

I wanted to say that I didn't want to talk to him but I couldn't say it.

"My sister said to give you this." He reached under his shirt and pulled out an Old Home bread sack and tossed it to me.

Through the plastic I saw a big slice of a yellow cake and a slice of angel food. I didn't know what to say. But before I could open my mouth, he turned the horse around and was galloping away. It was like having a fast car but the horse did the squealing and spinning.

I took the cake inside and looked at it and sniffed it. Cake, huh? I figured that Prudence was baking cakes to use up eggs. Aunt Kathy heard from the Fuller Brush man that Prudence made a puffy soufflé that was pretty when it came out of the oven in the round pan she'd made from a lard pail. She had a cookbook—*The Joy of Cooking*—that was missing a cover and pages from the front and back. She got it at a rummage sale for a quarter.

I showed the squashed cake to Dad and he didn't want to eat it. "Don't know where it's been," he said. "They don't even have beds."

"How do you know that?" I asked.

"Your Uncle Elmer told me. He said Aunt Kathy heard they slept on old mattresses on the floor."

"But their mom works and their dad, too. Why wouldn't they have money for beds?"

"'Cause they're gamblers. She's always at the VFW playing Bingo. Buys five cards at a time."

"How can she keep track of five?" I asked.

"I don't know but she does."

We didn't eat the cake. I'd taken a taste of the angel food and it wasn't sweet, like she forgot the sugar. It felt like foam—all full of air—just dry and plain. We threw it to Buster.

Dusty didn't show up for a week. I was getting used to his absence when I heard the horse's hooves on the road. And sure enough he was in the lane, throwing a bone to Buster. I opened the back door and there he was leaning down with a stick in his hand like he was trying to open the door with it.

"Was wondering if you'd like to go riding," he said.

"What do you mean riding?"

"On my horse. You know, you get on back behind me."

"You mean, you want me to get up there?" All I could think about was that I would have to hold onto him and put my hands on his waist. I'd have to be close to him and I'd eaten onions for lunch.

"Come on," he said.

I didn't know why but I nodded and asked, "How do I get on that thing?"

He told me to stand on the crossbar of the swing set and he would bring the horse to me. I stood on the bar and held onto the A frame while he brought the stallion right up beside me. He held the reins with one hand and reached out to me with the other. The horse was skittish and stepped away. Dusty had to bring him around again. "Now jump on as soon as I get there," he called out.

This time I let his arm reach out for mine and I lifted my leg and slid onto the bare back of the stallion. My legs spread apart and I wondered if I was hurting something I shouldn't be hurting. The horse's back felt hot and wet. Thank goodness I had on jeans, not shorts. I didn't want that hairy back against my skin.

"Grab around me and hold on."

I was embarrassed but I put my arms on his waist and realized how skinny he was. He was a stick with a head of sandy hair and smelled like the horse. He clicked with his tongue and the horse took off. I was jerked back and tightened my knees and hands. In the movies riders have a saddle to hold onto, but I had Dusty and he wasn't solid on this horse. He was bobbing and leaning forward like he didn't care if he fell. "Slow down," I said.

"Why? This is the best part. Wait until we really get moving."

"I want off," I said, but instead of stopping, the horse moved onto the road and I felt his body release and shoot forward. This horse was running full force and I held on as tight as I could. I had my arms all the way around Dusty's waist and my body was against his back. I'd never ever sat this close to a boy. I was flat against him, my breasts up against him. Thank God they were in a padded bra that added a cushion between him and them.

The horse was flying now. Its head was leaning forward, stretching like it wanted to make sure its head got there faster than its body. The gravel road beneath me seemed a long way down, and I knew he was purposely having this horse run to show off. I'd be killed if I fell.

The horse headed toward home and as he got nearer to the old Fogarty place he moved faster. I heard a car coming and Dusty called, "Hang on. He gets spooked."

And sure enough, the horse edged clear over to the rim of the road and when the car got closer, he headed down into the ditch. I felt better being closer to the sides of the ditch, but I worried about the horse catching its leg on barbed wire or stumbling in a badger hole.

Dusty was pulling back on the reins and leaning back. "Whoa, slow down boy. Slow down." And he was getting angry at the horse because it wasn't doing what he wanted it to do.

At the bend where the ditch was almost even with the road, the horse got back on the road and kept moving toward their place. He was out of control, that's for sure, and I closed my eyes and prayed. God, don't let me fall off. Once I get off this thing, I am not getting back on.

At their lane, Tyrone turned sharply and went so close to the fence post that I thought I was going to lose my leg. I had less than an inch or my leg would have been scraped against that wood.

I felt the horse slowing as it neared the barn. Dusty was pulling on the reins and saying, "Whoa, boy, whoa."

At the barn the horse came to an abrupt stop and I was smashed harder into Dusty's back. My chin dug into his shoulder and my hands reached for whatever was there and I grabbed too low on his jeans. I felt a bulge in his pants and let go.

The horse stood panting and I didn't even wait for him to find high ground so I could get off easily. I slid off the left side, since that was the side I got up on, and hit the ground with a thump, jumping away from the horse because I didn't want to get kicked.

I was so happy to be on the ground and away from that sweaty thing. I felt like crying but I didn't want Dusty to see.

Dusty slid off easily and I saw that he was excited as if he'd wanted this to happen all along. "Didn't you like that?"

"No," I said and moved to higher ground.

"Where you going?"

"Home."

"I'll give you a ride."

"No way. I'm not getting back on that horse."

I headed up the hill toward the house where chickens perched on the windowsills. The trailer was off near the grove where the Fogartys had kept the burn barrels. These new folks weren't too smart putting that trailer so close to the gooseberry bushes and shrubs where hordes of mosquitoes would get them.

I walked fast. Next thing I knew Prudence, her yellow hair slicked back in a ponytail, was standing at the door of the trailer leaning on the one railing attached to the steps. The other railing was missing. A window was also gone but pieces of cardboard boxes covered it. Duct tape ran back and forth across it.

"He does it on purpose," she called out.

I stopped for a second and turned to the steps. "Does what?"

"Makes Tyrone run like that. He does it all the time and then he almost rips your leg off on the post. Got mine two weeks ago." And she showed me a nasty red scrape with a long scab along the side of her leg.

"He just wants you to have to hang on tight to him. That's why he does it."

And I heard a voice behind me. "Shut your goddamn mouth."

"Shut yours," she said, flipping him the finger.

Dusty reached out and grabbed me by the shoulder. "I'll give you a ride. I'll make him canter."

"I said I'm walking."

"But I said I'd give you a ride." His face was contorted like I was really being mean to him by saying no.

I didn't answer him but walked faster. Then I began to run down their lane toward the road. I'd feel safer once on the road because that was my territory.

But he was behind me. "Come on. I'll make him go easy this time."

"Just leave me alone."

He turned and headed toward the barn. I kept running. I was on the road when I heard the sound of the horse. He was bringing it straight toward me. I ran into the ditch and up to the fence and climbed the barbed wire. I stood on the fence holding onto a post.

He was coming down into the ditch with the horse. "He'll go easy this time. It's just when he heads for the barn that he runs. He knows he's going home."

The horse was wet and had its ears back like it didn't want to be there.

"Stay there. You can get on his back from there."

But I jumped off the fence into the cornfield. "Just leave me alone." I dashed into the field about five feet. I remember Dad telling me that you should never go deep into a cornfield or they'd find your bones in fall when the picker ran over them.

I walked the sixth row, hoping he would go, but he kept the horse in the ditch parallel to me. I wanted to be left alone and wished I hadn't ever gotten on that horse with the creep. And how did I explain that bulge in his pants? I couldn't tell Dad.

Finally I came to the end of the field and a fence. I had to cross it and go into a pasture where there were cows. I was afraid of cows but I'd stay close to the fence. I felt trapped with Dusty and the stallion on one side and cows on the other. I wanted my dad to drive by and pick me up. At the fence, I rested against a post. I knew I had to keep going. I couldn't act scared.

I hurried along the fence, glancing back and forth—from cows to him. At the next fence I either had to walk across the Thorsen's open yard, and they had a mean dog, or I had to head down toward the river, crossing another fence into the timber. They kept a bull in there and I was afraid of bulls. If Dusty'd turn around and go back home, I could cross the gravel road to another field that would be better because it would go for another half mile—almost to my house.

Dusty came up close to the fence where I was. "Get on. Do you hear me? Quit acting like a stupid girl."

"I'm not getting on that horse again."

"Think you're so smart, huh. Well, I have you pinned down. You can't get home unless you cross that fence and I'm staying right here."

At that I heard a car and stood up on the fence, one foot on the post and the other on the top rung of the wire. It was the mail carrier and he never stopped to pick people up. My luck. I waved and he waved back but he didn't stop.

I didn't know what to do but I wasn't going to stay where I was and be trapped by a horse. I stayed in the cornfield and headed down toward the timber, but I had to cross another fence. Dusty wouldn't be able to follow me but I didn't want to run into the bull.

Keeping my eye on Dusty and looking for the bull, I walked into a thick grove of oaks. When I was in the trees I knelt down on the ground behind the largest oak. I wasn't going to go any further. I sat and waited. It had to be almost four o'clock. I should be getting supper ready but I was stuck.

It seemed forever until I saw Dusty turn the horse around and head for home, spurring the horse to gallop. At that I ran up the hill to the fence, crossed over, feeling like I was vulnerable in the open yard near the Thorsen's house. I raced across the gravel road, down into a ditch and up to the fence, which I climbed faster than I'd ever climbed a fence.

I ran and walked, keeping my eyes peeled and next thing I knew the dog was barking at Dusty and his horse, now over in the timber that I had just left. He had gone home, ridden down toward the river and made his way back into the timber, somehow getting across a fence. If I had been there, he would have galloped right up to me.

Inside I felt sick and ran harder down the row toward home. As I neared my place, I whistled for Buster. He heard me and came running toward me. I climbed over the fence and ran as fast as I could. I heard the horse's hooves on the road and about peed my pants. He was back. I dashed toward the mailbox but didn't stop to check it. Buster thought I was playing and tried to nip at my heels. I was at the back door when Dusty came charging into the lane. I slammed the door behind me and locked it. I heard Dusty yelling at Buster to shut up and I was so happy that he was doing his job.

I went to the front door that we never used and locked that.
I heard Dad's voice say, "What are you doing?"

"You're home. Why didn't you come looking for me?"

"What are you talking about?" Dad got out of his La-Z-Boy.

"I hate that kid. I hate him."

"What the hell happened? Did he do something to you?"

"He wouldn't let me get home unless I rode with him. And
I wouldn't do it and he kept following me." I broke down and cried.
I told him about Dusty and the horse and feeling stalked and trapped.
But I didn't tell him about the lump in his pants.

"Why the Sam Hill did you get on that horse with him?"

We saw Dusty outside in the lane trying to keep the horse still
but Buster kept barking. Dad opened the back door and walked out
toward him. As soon as Dusty saw him, he turned that horse around
and took off.

Dusty stayed away for a few weeks. But one day I was in the
kitchen baking cookies when I heard the back door open and I looked
to see what Dad was doing home. He was supposed to be helping
Elmer combine beans. I let out a small cry when it was Dusty and he
was standing right behind me. I could smell his sweat and egg breath.
I spun around.

"Don't you knock? You can't walk into someone's house like that."

"Just did," he said, smiling.

I didn't like that smile.

My timer buzzed and I had to take out the cookies. And he was
right there behind me as I reached into the oven. His leg brushed
against mine.

"What's happened between us?" he asked in a low voice.

And I felt his breath on my neck and wanted to slap him away.
I didn't answer him but leaned into the oven more. I turned around
with the hot cookie sheet and used that to keep him away from me.
I almost touched him with it. He acted like he didn't care if I
burned him.

"Get out of my way," my voice quivered. "I need to take these off before they stick."

I went to the table where I had a brown grocery sack that I had cut open and spread out. He followed me.

With the pancake spatula, I took the cookies off the sheet. He looked at those cookies like they were something foreign to him.

"I suppose you're too good for plain cookies. Some of us can't afford chocolate chips."

I didn't know what to say to that. He stepped closer to the table and with his hand pushed five cookies onto the floor. He laughed.

"Get out," I said, my voice nearly breaking.

"Not until you tell me why you won't go riding. It's me, isn't it? I'm not good enough for you?"

I felt nervous and sweaty. I wanted my dad home. "I just don't like horses."

"Do I scare you?" he asked in a strange low voice.

He did, but I didn't want to say anything. "No. Get real," I said, making a huffing noise.

"Then ride with me now. Come on."

"No," I said louder and my voice cracked.

"It's me. I seen you laugh at me when you're with that Janice. I seen it a lot."

"You don't know what you're talking about."

"Oh, I do. I know."

And with that he stormed out of the kitchen and kicked the door on the way out. I heard barking and Buster running after him. I saw him stop and turn to Buster and say something, then he reached down and grabbed a handful of gravel and tossed it at him. Buster growled and retreated.

I locked the back door and pushed a chair against it. My heart raced and I felt sick. I wanted to go get my dad but I was afraid to go outside and get in the pickup.

After that Dad gave me a ride to school for a week. But he got busy with harvesting and I had to ride the school bus again. I made sure that I sat in a spot where Dusty couldn't get near me. The driver

picked me up first and I looked for a place in front where I'd be at
the end of the seat and where people would be packed in behind
me. Then when Dusty and his sister got on, they would have to move
further back.

One day he stopped right at my seat and dropped a note in the
open book that I was reading. I refused to read the note while he
watched me. I just let it stay in that page and closed the book on it.
At school I ran to the women's restroom and opened the note. It said:
I'm always around, even when yur not looking.

I showed Janice and she said to show my dad. At home, Dad blew
up. "Who is this asshole? Next time you see him out there, you tell
me." And Dad went down to the basement and opened the door to
his gun cabinet. He picked out his deer-hunting shotgun and cocked
it and looked into the chamber. He was acting like one of the pioneers
who was going after Inkpaduta.

"Dad, you can't use that."

"Who says I can't?"

I didn't know if I was more afraid for my dad and what he'd do,
or for me.

But Dusty never showed up again when Dad was home.
Sometimes I felt he had a view of our place. I couldn't figure out how
he could know unless he was out there in the ditch or in our barn loft.

One Saturday morning five minutes after Dad'd driven out the
lane, Dusty came riding in on Tyrone and he threw Buster a bone.

I locked the doors and went upstairs so I could watch from high
up. He came up to the kitchen window and knocked on it. "I know
you're in there. Come on out and ride with me."

On the bus on Monday, he stopped by my seat and dropped
another note into my book. It said: *I know you're in there watching me
when I come by. If you don't open that door, I'm going to break it down.*

That was it. Dad took the note to the sheriff and the sheriff drove
up to the O'Leary place and warned Dusty that he'd better leave me
alone or he would arrest him for trespassing.

Dad stayed home more and when he'd be gone, he had me go
over to Janice's or I'd have her over. On another Saturday when Janice

had spent the night and Dad was out corn picking for the day, Janice and I saw Dusty darting from building to building. We went upstairs to watch him. We moved from Dad's window to my window to the bathroom window.

"I don't like this," Janice said. She was a big chicken.

"We're inside. He can't get in."

"Let's go to my house. Your pickup's out there. Come on." My dad had taken the tractor to Elmer's place.

So we got our purses and ran out the door heading for the pickup. Once in, we locked the doors. I didn't see Buster and was mad that that dog was worthless. A traitor—all for a stupid bone.

We drove to Janice's house and told her mother that Dusty was sneaking around my place. She called the sheriff and told him we'd meet him there in twenty minutes. She had us follow her in the pickup.

The sheriff was already at the back door that was open and the window was broken.

"Someone broke in while you were gone. I want you to check if anything's stolen."

I followed the sheriff into the house. Janice and her mother were behind me. We walked slowly and the sheriff had his hand on his gun. He led the way. We walked through the kitchen and living room. Then we went to the basement which we didn't keep too clean. We threw all our stuff down there. I was embarrassed having them see this mess and then they even saw where Dad showered. There was a toilet in the basement and Dad kept a pile of magazines down there with a roll of toilet paper sitting right on top of the pile.

After looking down there, we went upstairs to my bedroom. The sheriff stopped at my bedroom door.

"Got quite a mess in here, Miss."

Janice and I both crammed in beside him. One dresser drawer was pulled out and underwear was on the bed and floor. My scissors, which I kept on the dresser, were gone and some of my underpants were cut in half. But the worst was that Dusty had found my box of Kotex and cut them in pieces and had thrown them all over my bed. His dirty hands had been in my box of pads. And I saw a piece of paper in the empty drawer. I went over and opened it. It said: *I'm gonna get you. You ain't stopping me.*

And then Janice found another one and it said: *Suck my cock.* She let it drop and the sheriff picked it up. "Whoever did this should have his mouth washed out."

"It's Dusty's writing," I said. It was like the other notes that he'd handed me on the bus.

Janice's mother was making all sorts of noises. "Oh my, you girls shouldn't be reading those things. What kind of kid is he?"

"He's a pervert, Ma'am. That's all there is to it," the sheriff said.

My red nail polish had been opened up and some of it poured onto a pad but most of it was on top of the dresser making a puddle. It was dried and I'd never get it off.

A school photo that I had taped to my mirror was marked up with my black magic marker. He'd drawn four circles around my face, making a bull's-eye right between my eyes. "Gosh, does he want to shoot you or something?" said Janice.

"Just trying to act tough, that's what he's doing." The sheriff took that, too.

I felt sick and dirty. I wanted to burn everything that he touched. My room wasn't mine anymore.

The sheriff found two more notes but he wouldn't let me read them. He said they weren't fit for our eyes. But I was angry with him for hiding them from me. I should be able to read them. It was my room and they were written to me. The sheriff said he wanted to take some pictures so he went to his car and came back with a camera. He took six photos as evidence. Then he took all the notes and said he'd use them, too.

I thought, all this just because I wouldn't accept a ride home on his stupid horse. All this because I didn't want to talk to him.

My dad came home when the sheriff was taking the last picture.

"What the hell is this?" my dad said when he came up the stairs and saw all of us in my bedroom.

"Got some young pup who doesn't understand he can't break into a girl's house and write her nasty messages." And the sheriff handed my dad the notes. "He put them in her drawers, you know where she keeps her private things."

Why couldn't he say underwear? He made it seem like I was doing something bad.

I watched my dad's face turn red. First it was his ears and then it was his neck and his nose. He began to rip the notes but the sheriff put his hand out. "No, we need evidence."

"I don't want anyone to see these. I just want that son of a bitch out of my neighborhood. I never trusted him from the get-go. Knew he was nothing but trouble."

The sheriff tried to calm Dad down and soon we were all moving downstairs.

Before he left, the sheriff said, "You can go ahead and clean that room, but if you find any more notes let me know."

Janice and her mom waited around a bit. "Do you need help cleaning up?" Mrs. Larson asked.

"Nope," my dad said. "Don't need no help. She'll do it."

They could tell that my dad didn't want them around or anyone around. He was burning mad.

When they were out the door and into their car, my dad turned to me. "I told you not to ride with that boy. Look at what happened."

"Don't you go blaming me. I didn't know he was that weird."

"I told you. Don't you remember? I said he was horsey people and you've got to stay away from them."

"Well, I didn't make him do this."

Dad began moving toward the stairs and toward my room. I followed. At the door, he said again. "Jesus Christ. Thinks he can come in here and wreck our stuff. Has no respect for property, but what can you expect? Look where they live."

My dad grabbed my wastebasket but when he saw that he would have to pick up Kotex pads, he handed it to me.

"Get this mess out of here."

He stood there and I said, "You're making it seem like I wanted this. I didn't." And I began to cry. My dad didn't know what to do. He stepped toward me and it looked like he was going to reach out but he pulled his hands back, rubbing them together. "I'm going to go down there right now and give that kid a piece of my mind."

"Don't, Dad. The sheriff's doing that."

"Well, I have to do something, don't I? Ain't I supposed to do something because I'm your dad?"

"I don't know."

"Well, it just seems like he took liberties that he ain't supposed to take."

"That's for sure."

And then Dad turned on me and looked at me. "You sure he didn't do anything to you when you were riding with him? Did he touch you or something?"

"No, but his thing was big."

"Was it out of his pants?"

"No, Dad. When the horse stopped, I grabbed there by mistake. It was just big, you know, in front."

"What the hell. I just knew it. Goddamn."

"But he didn't do anything."

"Didn't do anything? Look at this and look at the broken window downstairs and those notes."

"I mean, like touching me."

"Well, I ain't leaving you home alone anymore."

"Dad, I'm sixteen. I've been home alone for years. You can't be here every minute. Geez, I'm not a baby."

"Judas priest, I know that. But it was easier when you were." He reached out with both hands and grabbed my shoulders like he was ready to shake me and remind me how much easier it was when I was little, and then he let go. He let his hands drop and stormed down the stairs and headed outside. I watched as he went toward the shed where he kept junk he collected. Soon I saw him with a roll of snow fencing that the county road crew had forgotten to pick up last spring. And sure enough he was headed toward the lane. For an hour he worked making a fence across our lane. I knew he'd just have to take it down tomorrow when he had to leave. But for some strange reason putting up that stupid snow fence was making him feel better.

Half-blood

1968

*I*t was a late spring. Dad got plenty of work helping with plowing and disking, and I waited for the land to turn green. Sometimes I'd make Janice go walking with me even though she didn't want to. She'd heard that the ghosts of Inkpaduta roamed the riverbanks. We'd fill a jar full of water and take off heading down the river toward Emmetsburg. Maybe I was enjoying the spring more because I knew that the next one I'd be away at college.

I felt like I had to get so many things done in order to leave. Last summer we'd painted the outside of the house white and the front door forest green. The front steps were crumbling so we put in new cement steps with railings. And the cement truck returned a week later and poured a driveway in front of the back door and garage. We looked like town people with our cement. Janice and I would take kitchen chairs and just sit out there. It felt like we had a patio.

It was a month away from graduation when on a Friday late afternoon I looked out toward the road and saw a girl walking with a duffel bag on her shoulders. I went outside to the front step to get a better look. Buster saw her and began running toward the end of the lane. I called out and whistled for him to come back.

The girl stopped on the road and didn't move. I walked out the
lane and reached for Buster's collar. Once she saw I held him by his
collar, she walked toward me. She came closer, stopping about ten feet
away from me. "You're not going to let him go, are you?"

"That depends," I said, "on what you're going to do."

"I'm not doing anything but looking for a girl name Brigid."

My eyes narrowed and I looked closer at her. Her brown hair was
stringy and dirty and she had it tucked behind each ear. She had gold
hoops in each ear. Her blue jeans had a piece of braid sewn to the
bottom but the braid was dirty and dragging on the gravel. She had an
army jacket on that was way too big for her. Around each eye she had
black lines.

"What if I said I was Brigid?"

"Then I'm here and that man told me right."

"What man?"

"Some farmer who gave me a ride part way. He said to walk a few
miles and I'd find you."

"And who are you?" I asked, but I already knew.

"Don't you know?"

I didn't think she'd look this old already. She'd grown three or
four inches since I last saw her. "Are you from Florida?"

She smiled. "Yah, I'm Justine, your sister." And when she smiled
I saw she had small teeth in front, and one was discolored—sort of
brown—like it was dead. Her mouth looked young.

"What are you doing here?"

"Just wanted to see you."

"How'd you get here?"

"Took the bus."

I stood up and let go of Buster's collar. She instantly ran toward
me and held onto my arm. "I don't like dogs. You've got to hold him."

I couldn't believe she was holding onto my arm. She was skinny
as all get-out and shorter than me by a couple of inches. And she'd
didn't smell so good—sort of yeasty and sweaty and smoky like she
had a cigarette.

"If you stay right next to me, then Buster will leave you alone."

I really wanted her to keep holding onto my arm. So we walked
together and she never took her eyes off Buster, who had run ahead.

As we neared the house, she said, "This is yours? It's nicer than
I remember."

"We just painted it last August," I said.

"Did you paint?"

"Yah, me and Dad did."

"Where is he?" she said, looking around.

"He's plowing for his brother Elmer."

I brought her in the side door to the kitchen. We called it the back
door but it was on the side. She seemed relieved to be inside and she
let go of my arm and looked around at the cupboards and stuff.

"Want a cookie?" I asked. I opened the lid to the cookie jar and
held it out to her. She took one and shoved it in her mouth.

I watched her walk into the living room and look around. I was
so glad that Dad and I had fixed it up two winters ago. It was a comfy
room with a new couch and chair and coffee table.

She stood there turning around and around looking at the room
and then walking back into the kitchen.

"Want to take a bath?" I asked. I noticed she smelled more when
we were inside the house.

"Where is it?"

"Upstairs," I nodded toward the door to the stairs.

I led the way and she followed. At my bedroom door I paused.
I hadn't made my bed and the room looked messy. I went over to
the bed and pulled up the sheets and bedspread. It always looked so
much better once the bed was smooth and everything tucked in.

She dropped her army duffel bag on the floor and said, "This is
yours, all yours, isn't it?"

"Well, yes, there's no other kid in the house. My dad's room is
next door."

She walked over to the dresser and picked up my Chantilly
perfume bottle and sniffed it. I pulled off the lid and picked up her
hand. I pushed back the sleeve to spray her wrist and when I did that
I saw she had all sorts of things drawn on her arms and hands, like she

had taken a ballpoint pen and made designs and words. I saw the
F word. "You have to wash that off. My dad will really be mad it he
sees that."

She shrugged and sniffed the cologne. "I like the bottle. It's
so pink."

With her other hand, she reached for a bottle of Avon Skin So
Soft and sniffed that.

"I'll put some in your bath water. You'll feel silky all over."

"Where's the bathtub?" she asked.

I took her into our bathroom that had a new sink and mirror and
wallpaper. My aunt Kathy had helped me wallpaper it last summer.
I really liked the red-and-white-designed paper. Dad had some guy
who owed him money help him put in a white piece of linoleum. It
looked clean. We painted all the trim on the window and door white.
I bought white towels and a rug at JC Penney's.

"I'll fill the tub for you."

I moved to the tub and put in the rubber plug. It was a big old
claw-leg tub but I never filled it to the top. Dad got mad if I wasted
that much water. I turned on the water.

"I do my hair in here. I use this to rinse it." I showed her a plastic
pitcher that I filled with water and poured over my head.

She just stood there watching me do everything. I helped her pull
off her jacket and saw she had on a black tee shirt.

"Are you going to be okay? Do you need help?" I asked.

"Jesus Christ, I made it all the way here from Florida. I think I can
do it myself."

I was stung by her words and backed off.

When she dropped her coat on the floor, I picked it up and saw
an almost empty cigarette package in the top pocket. I hung it on the
hook on the back of the bathroom door.

"Do you need to borrow some clean clothes?" I tried to keep my
voice sweet.

"No, I have clothes in my bag."

She walked back to my room and untied the duffle bag. She
rummaged around and pulled out another tee shirt and jeans and

I was hoping another pair of underpants. Maybe she had them in that bundle she took into the bathroom.

I sat on the bed and listened to her get into the tub. I heard her splash and turn on the water again. After it ran for a while, I started getting worried. What if she overflowed the tub? Dad would kill me.

I knocked on the door. "Justine, turn off the water. Our hot water heater doesn't hold much."

I waited but she didn't turn it off.

"Justine, are you asleep or something?" I called out.

"Okay, okay. Just leave me alone," she answered.

"Not until you turn off that water."

Finally I heard her turn off the faucets. I felt relief. I wished she hadn't locked the door. What if she drowned in there? I'd have to break down the door.

I went back and sat on the bed and waited. It felt so strange having her here. I walked over to her duffel bag and looked inside. I saw clothes just stuffed in there. They were mostly dark colors. I reached inside and felt something hard; it was a flashlight. I thought I heard her splashing and I pulled my hand out, afraid she might open the door and see me.

When she came out of the tub, she looked twelve. She had washed all the black stuff from around her eyes and her hair was wet and stringy. She went to her bag and dug around until she pulled out a plastic sack filled with stuff. She pulled out a brush and a black pencil. She stood in front of my mirror and drew lines around each eye.

"Why do you do that?" I asked.

"Because I want to."

"But it makes you look older and scarier," I said.

She smiled. "I want to look older."

"What about scarier? Do you want people to be afraid of you?"

"That's okay with me."

I watched her brush through her long hair. Her bangs were long and hung below her eyes. She didn't seem to mind that they were covering her face. I walked over and took the brush from her.

"I'll do it for you," I said.

"I can do it myself."

"I know, but it's something sisters do for each other. Haven't you read any books or watched any movies where they brush each other's hair?"

I pulled her back to sit on the edge of the bed and I sat behind her slowly brushing through her hair. She should have rinsed it better but I didn't say anything.

"Why did you come here?" I asked.

"I hated my foster home."

"Where's our mom?"

Justine gave me a how-can-you-be-so-stupid look that I could see in the mirror. "Where do you think?"

"I don't know."

"She's out there drinking and drugging again. She was supposed to come and visit me last month but she didn't show. No one knows where she is."

"Does she have a boyfriend?" I asked quietly.

"Boyfriends. The last guy wore a stupid cowboy hat and had a silver belt like he'd stolen it from Indians. And he was old."

"Well, that's only one guy," I said defending her.

"On the Fourth of July she showed up with two guys who looked real young. One guy was chewing bubble gum and had zits all over his face."

Justine walked to the duffel bag, sat down on the floor, and began pulling out clothes. She came to a paperback book without a cover. Inside it there was picture. She handed it to me. I sat down on the floor next to her.

It was a picture of Mom with Justine. A Christmas tree decorated in all red balls and red fringy stuff was behind them. A few unopened presents were on the floor. Mom's blonde hair was long and flat and she had sunglasses pushed back on her head. She was holding a cigarette in one hand and holding Justine's hand in the other. I hated to see this. I hated having her hold her hand. Why couldn't it be mine?

"What'd she give you?" I asked.

"A tube of chapstick and a paperback book that they took away from me."

"Why?" I asked.

"'Cause it wasn't appropriate for my age. I think it had dirty words and sex stuff in it. Mom picked it up at some truck stop. She didn't even wrap it."

"Where'd you get that book?" I pointed to the one she held in her hand.

"My foster mom gave it to me. It's *To Kill a Mockingbird*, but the cover fell off. I've read it three times. I'd like a dad like that Atticus Finch."

"Who is your dad?"

"Don't know much other than he was Mexican. That's why I'm darker than you. I got more of him in me than Mom."

"What was his name?"

"Mom called him Cheeser because he liked cheese pizza."

"What about his last name?"

"Don't know that. My birth certificate says my father was unknown. I have the same last name as you do. Don't you think that's strange?"

"You have the same last name?"

"Yah, my mom said he turned mean on her and she didn't want him to ever get his hands on me. But that seems stupid now considering I don't have her either."

"Her hair's real blonde," I said, motioning to the photo.

"She bleaches it."

"Do you think she's pretty?" I asked softly.

"No, she's a mess. Her face is wrinkled and she's always shaking."

"But she looks okay here," I said.

"She was prettier when she wasn't drinking. When she was working everyday and getting sleep at night, she looked better."

At that I heard Buster barking. I jumped up and went to the window. I saw my dad driving in the lane in the pickup. "My dad's home. Boy, will he be surprised." I knew that he would be mad and pouty again. Whenever I mentioned my mother, he refused to talk.

I handed the picture back to her and she put it in the book and shoved it into the duffel bag.

When he walked in the door, he called out, "I'm home."

We always did this. We told each other when we were leaving and when we were home. I didn't know whether to take her downstairs or wait for him to come upstairs. But I didn't have to decide. He came up the stairs; I saw his head through the railings.

When he was in the hallway, he saw her. He stopped and looked confused.

"Dad, you'll never guess who showed up this afternoon."

"Who?" he asked, looking like he did when that skunk came loping into the lane and he studied it before getting out his gun.

"Justine, you know, my sister."

He stopped.

Justine turned around to face him. She mumbled hello or something.

I just watched my dad.

"How'd she get here?" he asked quietly.

"She took the bus."

"And when's she leaving?"

"Dad!"

"I want to know. Did her mother send her?"

Justine stood up. "No, she didn't. I came on my own. I'm going to live with you guys."

My dad looked like he'd been punched a good one in the stomach and I held my breath. "I wouldn't be so sure about that, young lady."

"Dad, be nice," I warned.

"Weren't you in some home?" Dad asked.

"A foster home. And I ain't going back."

"So you ran away. Did you tell them where you were going?"

"No, I don't want them to know."

"Well, we're going to have to tell the sheriff. They're probably looking for you."

When Justine heard that, she walked over to her duffel bag and began to shove the clothes down into it.

"What are you doing?" I asked.

"I'm not going back there."

I felt myself well up with fear and panic. I couldn't lose her. She was right here in front of me. I'd brushed her hair and I wasn't going to have her take off.

"Dad, how could you!"

Dad looked at me like I was crazy. "Could what?"

I gave him my squinty-eye look. "She's tired and needs rest. We can't let her walk away. Can she stay the night?"

Dad paused. "Just one night. We'll get in trouble ourselves if we harbor a criminal."

"I'm no criminal. I'm family."

At that there was silence. He didn't seem to know what to say and he just stood there outside my door for a second before he left.

She looked at me. "What should I do?" she whispered.

"That means you can spend the night," I said.

"It does?" She looked from me to the steps that Dad had just gone down.

"Yup, it does."

I went over to her and eased the duffel bag from her shoulder. "Let's go make supper, okay?"

She nodded. "I know how to cook. Been doing it since I was little."

We walked downstairs together. I wanted to put my arm on her shoulder but I thought she might get mad at that. She didn't seem like the type of kid who liked to be touched.

In the kitchen, I saw that the basement door was ajar. Dad was down there taking a shower. I went to the cupboard and opened it. "Do you want spaghetti or hamburgers?"

"Spaghetti," she said.

And I pulled out the package of noodles and a can of Hunt's sauce. I had hamburger thawed out. "We can make meatballs," I said.

She nodded.

In a bowl I mixed hamburger, breadcrumbs, and an egg.

"Why do you use an egg?" she asked.

"It keeps it sticking together," I said.

"At my first foster home, I had to fix one meal a week.
I made nachos."

"I've never made them but I have made tacos."

Justine was looking in the cupboard. "How come you have three
sets of dishes?"

"Somebody paid Dad with a set of dishes once. Then we won
another set at the Farm and Home Store opening and that other one
is our mom's. I wouldn't let him give them away."

"You mean, the ones that look like pottery?"

"Yup."

"I can't believe Mom ever lived here. It's too quiet for her."

"What do you mean?"

Justine had taken a plate out and was looking at it. "Just that.
Mom never stayed home. Always had to be out where there were
lots of people."

"You mean in bars," Dad added, coming through the basement
door in a clean tee shirt and jeans. His bare feet left wet marks on
the linoleum.

Justine stopped and looked at him, not saying anything.

"Dad, just quit it," I said.

"Well, it's true. Bars were more her home, not this place," said Dad.

There was a loud noise and we turned to see the plate on the floor
in pieces.

"They're our plates now, not hers," said Dad. "You don't have to
break them."

Justine just stood there looking at the pieces; her head hung
down. I expected her to be crying but when I went over to help pick
up the pieces, she kneeled down next to me and smiled at me. I was so
surprised and I couldn't smile back. I was upset about the plate. I had
been so careful with them all these years.

"Did it slip out of your hand?" I asked.

She shrugged and just sat there squatting next to me, watching
me pick up the larger pieces.

"Well, help me. Get that broom over there." I pointed to the
broom hanging from a nail by the door to the basement.

I had put a leather tie through the handle so we could hang it.

Dad reached for the broom and handed it to Justine. "Here. I'm not going over there or I'll cut my feet."

Justine did the strangest thing. She looked at Dad and said, "I'm not your fucking slave," and turned and walked up the stairs.

I never said that word in this house and Dad usually didn't either. We both watched her walk away.

"That's it. I'm calling the sheriff. I won't have that kind of talk in my house."

"Just wait. She's upset."

"I don't care if she's upset. She can't talk that way."

I grabbed the broom and swept the pieces into the dustpan.

"Dad, fry these meatballs," I said.

"Let me get some shoes on."

I turned and went upstairs to check on her. When I got to the top of the stairs, I saw her sitting on my bed with my two pillows propped behind her, looking in my scrapbook and chewing gum. She'd taken the gum from the new pack that was in my purse. My purse was open on the dresser with stuff spilling out.

I wanted to ask her why she broke the plate but I was afraid to. I didn't want her to leave. "Are you coming down to help me with supper?"

"Why do you call it supper? That sounds like you're a hick."

"That's what we call it here."

"Who are these two?" she asked, pointing to a picture.

I knew what picture she was talking about. "The McGinty girls."

"Jesus Christ, they think they're something, don't they?"

"They're my friends," I said quietly.

She turned another page. "We have a lot prettier queens in Florida. At my third home, my foster sister was runner-up for Miss Florida."

"Are you coming down to help me or not?"

"Not. You go ahead and call me when it's ready."

I paused. "What are you going to do?"

"I like looking through all your stuff."

"Well, I don't want you to do that without me up here."

She lowered the scrapbook and looked at me. "What's with you?"

"Nothing's with me. It's just that you can't go getting into my stuff without asking."

"Do you think I'm going to steal it?"

"I didn't say that, but you didn't ask to look at that or to chew my gum," I said.

"Oh God, you sound like my foster mother, always so full of rules."

I watched her toss the scrapbook on the bed and get up. She walked out the door and said, "Go ahead. Check out if I stole anything. That's what they all do."

I didn't know what to say, so I left the scrapbook on the bed. I didn't want to check the room and have her think I was like her foster mother.

I followed her down the stairs. Dad was frying the meatballs at the stove and she went over to the table and sat down. She just sat there with her hands folded in front of her and looked at the wall.

I was afraid to ask her to do anything. I got three plates from the cupboard and took them over to the table. She just stayed in the same spot while I set the table. I had to put the plate off to the side because she wouldn't move her hands.

Dad gave me a funny look when I walked over to the stove to put the spaghetti into the boiling water.

It seemed like it took forever for that spaghetti to cook.

"How did you get out to our place?" Dad asked her. He didn't like the silence.

Justine didn't answer him.

He looked at me. "How'd she get here?"

"She got a ride to the bridge and walked the rest of the way."

"That's a long walk," Dad said.

Still there was no response from her. When finally I carried the bowl of spaghetti and meatballs over to the table, I saw that she had her eyes closed.

I motioned to Dad and he shrugged his shoulders.

"Supper's ready," he said loudly and we watched her eyes open.

We sat down on each side of her and Dad and I made the sign of the cross and said grace together. Her eyes moved back and forth from Dad and then to me.

"Why do you do that?" she asked when we were through.

"You mean, say grace?" I asked.

"No, that thing with touching your head and shoulders. Looks like something witches do."

Dad's eyes narrowed. "It's not any witch stuff. It's the sign of the cross and that's enough with the questions. Just eat." Dad's voice was sharp, maybe too sharp because when we passed the bowl to her she passed it right on to me.

"Aren't you eating?"

"Don't eat meat."

"Well, why didn't you say something?"

She shrugged.

"Don't take a meatball then," Dad said.

"It's in the sauce. It's got meat juice in it already."

"At this house we eat what's put on the table," Dad said.

"I eat peanut butter. And I know you have it. I saw it in the cupboard," she said to me, turning away from Dad.

"Do you want it?" I asked.

She nodded and jumped up and walked to the cupboard. She knew exactly where it was. She grabbed the loaf of bread that was near the toaster and carried both of them back to the table.

Dad ate fast. I could tell he didn't want to be there with her.

I tried to eat my spaghetti carefully since she was at the table. Usually I didn't mind if I slurped up the long noodles. But I felt I had to be an example to her.

I watched her put the chunky peanut butter on the bread and take a huge bite. She took a drink of milk to wash it down. She seemed to thoroughly enjoy the peanut butter. She made smacking noises with her tongue and mouth. Dad looked at her a few times and seemed to almost say something but he didn't. And I was mad at her for not telling us she didn't like meatballs. We'd scurried around trying to make them for her and she didn't want them in the first place.

Dad ate two helpings and then left the table to go watch TV.
I waited for a while at the table but she was so slow. She was chewing
like she had all day. When I saw her take another piece of bread and
slather more peanut butter on it, I began to clear off the table.

She seemed to be in another world.

"Can you help dry the dishes?" I asked her after I had washed the
plates and cups.

"I like it when they drip dry. Just let them sit there and they'll
be okay."

I stopped. "No, we dry them and put them away in this house.
Here." I handed her a dishtowel. She didn't seem to want to dry them
and she took one plate and spent a minute on it. Then she took a
glass and spent a lot of time stuffing most of the towel inside it and
twisting the glass around and around. It made squeaking noises. It
was slow going.

"You spend a lot of time on one glass," I said.

"Hey, I'm doing it the best way I know how. If you want to do
them, I'll just quit."

"You can't quit until you're done," I said.

She smiled at me. "I'm done," she said and dropped the towel on
the floor and walked up the stairs.

Dad came in from the living room where he must have overheard
her and pointed to the towel on the floor. "I'm calling the sheriff. She's
nothing but a trouble maker and I don't want her around."

I was torn. For years I had told Dad we should let her stay with
us and now I wasn't so sure. When I went upstairs, she was in my bed,
under the covers, sleeping. Her clothes were in a pile on the floor. She
looked naked. And she was taking up the whole bed. Her face seemed
softer when she slept. It was missing the smirk and bored look. She
had her head on one pillow and she was holding onto my other pillow,
hugging it like it was a stuffed bear. I would have to borrow one of
Dad's pillows tonight and try to take that one she was holding away
from her. I couldn't sleep without two pillows.

When I went downstairs, I told Dad that she was already asleep.
"Maybe she was just tired, maybe that's why she was s—."

"Such a smart ass," Dad finished.

"When I get really tired, I get crabby."

"I think she's a smart ass all the time. I tell you I don't want her here."

"Let her stay one more day. Please. She'll be better after she's slept."

"Why are you so set on keeping her?"

"Because she's my sister."

"She's only your half sister."

"Still, she's blood."

Dad was standing at the kitchen sink, holding onto the edge with his hands. "Well, not very good blood. She's half your mother and I think she got all the bad parts of her. But then I don't know that there's any good parts to that woman."

"Don't say that. Because I'm part of her too and that makes me feel like you think I'm bad."

"I didn't say that."

"You did too."

"I know you've got more of me in you. That's why you're okay," he said.

"Okay, huh."

"And you don't have spic blood in you like she does. You can see it in her shifty eyes."

"You're a bigot."

He spun around. "I'm what?"

"You heard me. You're a bigot."

"What's that?"

"You know, you're a redneck—you're a prejudiced redneck."

"Well, I didn't abandon you or leave you in some foster home. I did my duty. And my duty is to you—not some spic foster kid who runs away and dresses like some devil worshipper."

I couldn't believe this was my father saying these things. "She's not a devil worshipper."

"And how do you know?"

"And the same goes for you—how do you know?" I screamed.

"She put her hands over her ears when we prayed and she has

those black lines around her eyes and that black tee shirt has a sign
of Satan on it."

"A sign of Satan. You've gone wacko."

"No, I'm not. I read about it in *Newsweek*. I'll show you."

And Dad stormed into the living room to rummage through
the pile of magazines on the coffee table. He was leafing through the
pages when he came back in. "Look at this. He pointed to a sign. Go
look at her shirt."

I ran upstairs to the pile of clothes and pulled out the tee shirt.
It had the sign.

When I turned around, he was at my door, nodding at me and
pointing to the magazine in his hand.

I put my finger to my mouth to tell him to be quiet and I pushed
him ahead of me and pulled the door closed. I was surprised she
hadn't heard us and woken up.

He turned to me on the stairs. "See. It's on the shirt."

"Someone might have given her the shirt. I wear tee shirts Janice
gives me and I don't pay any attention to what's on them."

"I bet she pays attention."

"I'm going to bed," I told Dad before he went back downstairs.

I was quiet getting into my pajamas and I decided to push her
over to her side and take back my pillow. I found my stuffed bear and
made a switch. I took the pillow from her arms and put the bear there.
She only made a moan when I did that.

I slipped into the bed and felt the warm spot where she had been
lying. I was careful not to touch her but I couldn't help but feel like
this was unreal. For years I'd dreamed of us sharing a room and bed
together. Janice had to share her bed with her sister and when I stayed
overnight her sister went to the couch.

I smelled the peanut butter still on her breath, and other smells.
She had an unfamiliar smell, sort of sour and sweet at the same time.
In the light from the hall coming in the crack in my door, I saw her
face. The black around her eyes was smudged and she looked like she
had deep bags. I wanted to tell her to quit putting that black pencil
on herself. And maybe if she wore something besides black she might

look like she was nicer and talk and act nicer. I planned how I would change her—make her into a decent kid. I would begin tomorrow.

I inched my foot over and felt her leg. She didn't move. She seemed to be out of it but I figured she was tired from the long bus trip and the walk to our place. It was nice being with her when she was silent. She didn't seem so bratty then. I must have lain there for an hour thinking how I'd give her two of the drawers in the dresser and hang up the rest of my clothes to make room.

I fell asleep and the next thing I knew, Dad was shaking me. "Brigid, wake up," he whispered.

"What time is it?"

"Four o'clock."

All I could think of was that it was Saturday and I could sleep late.

"Come in the bathroom," he said.

So I pulled myself out of bed and went to him. He was in the bathroom with the medicine chest open.

"Did you take my pills?" he asked.

"Why would I take your pills?"

"I don't know. The bottle's empty."

He opened the amber bottle and showed me that it was empty. "I had six or seven left."

"Were those your sinus pills?"

"No, muscle relaxers. My back's bothering me again."

And then he looked at the other bottles and they were all empty. He even checked the aspirin bottle, and it was empty too.

We both looked at each other. And it took me awhile to register what was happening.

"She was in here before you got home. She took a bath."

"Damn. She took them," he said.

"But why?"

"I bet she's got her mom's problem."

"She's too young."

Dad was in his boxer shorts. He never wore pajamas. "Seven-year-olds can be addicts, so she isn't too young."

"How do you know that?"

"It said in *Newsweek*."

"Do you think we'd better wake her?"

"Can you hear her breathing?"

We had moved to the door of my room. We were quiet as we listened to her. I could hear her shallow breathing. "She's alive," I said.

"God, I hope so."

"Should we wake her?"

With that we heard her turn over and then we saw her sit up in bed. "What are you two mumbling about?" she said.

"Hey, Missy, I want my pills."

"Don't know what you're talking about."

Dad turned on the light and walked into my room. He lifted the duffel bag and poured the contents on the floor. She jumped out of bed in her red underpants. She was flatter than a pancake so she didn't need a bra.

I saw my bottle of pearl nail polish roll out and my First Communion rosary and the picture of Mom's kitchen band that used to be on the wall. I looked at the wall to the spot where it had been. I hadn't even noticed it was gone.

"Find those pills, dammit," Dad said.

She knelt down and found the dirty pair of jeans she'd taken off. In the pocket she pulled out a plastic sack that was full of pills. She threw it at Dad. It hit his bare chest and landed at his feet.

"Missy, you're out of here in the morning. I'm calling the sheriff."

"Oh yah, I'll leave before he gets here."

"No, you're not." And Dad scooped up all the clothes and her boots and stuffed them back in the duffel bag. I knelt down and got my stuff. I was angriest about the kitchen band picture in the frame I found at the Osgood dump. The crack in the corner had gotten larger.

"Get her clothes by the bed," Dad motioned.

Justine got back in bed and just laughed. "Think you're so smart, huh? Well, I've gotten out of more foster homes than you know. You ain't going to stop me from leaving."

Dad and I didn't say anything. I think I just stood there with my mouth open. I didn't understand this kind of kid. I really wanted to sleep in my own bed but she was there and I was too mad at her to get back in with her.

I followed Dad as he carried the duffel bag into his room. Things kept falling and I had to pick them up. Dad opened his closet and threw the bag in there. Then he pushed his dresser in front of the door.

Dad had the sack of pills in his hand and I saw him go into the bathroom. He looked through the sack and pulled out a small green one. He put the sack back into the medicine cabinet.

"Better not leave that, Dad," I said.

"You're right." He took the sack into his bedroom.

I took a pillow from his bed and a quilt from the linen closet and went downstairs to the couch.

It took me awhile to go to sleep. I was so angry at her for taking my stuff. I had been nice to her, let her sleep in my bed, and I'd have to wash all the bedding once she left.

Dad was awake by six o'clock and calling the sheriff. He wanted to make sure the sheriff was there before she got out of bed. I smelled the coffee and heard Dad roaming around in the kitchen. I could tell he was eating cereal by the sound of the spoon hitting the sides of the bowl.

When Buster began barking, I got up. The sheriff's official car was out front. "Better get her up and have her get dressed."

"I can't open your closet door," I said.

Dad went upstairs and pushed back the dresser. I pulled out the bag and carried it to my room. When I walked in, she was gone. I was about to say something when I heard the toilet flush. She walked back into my room, wearing my good tee shirt and carrying her army jacket.

"Take that off and put on your own clothes," I said.

"Aren't you going to give me something to remember you by?" she asked.

"Why should I?"

She just shrugged and rummaged through her duffel bag. I watched her pull out another black tee shirt. She let mine drop to the floor and put on hers. She dug into the duffel again and then tossed me my bottle of Chantilly cologne.

"How much more of my stuff is in there?"

I heard my dad calling up. "Bring her down."

I felt like I was bringing a prisoner down to him. In my desk I had a packet of school photos—pictures from many years. I handed her one but she took the whole envelope and looked through them. She picked out three and put them in the pocket of her green army jacket next to the package of cigarettes.

I watched her stuff everything down into that bag. Nothing was folded. It was just like clothes when they came out of the dryer but worse.

"Why did you take my stuff?" I asked again.

"You got so much that you won't miss it."

"Yes, I would. My mom's kitchen band picture is real important to me."

"So you got it back."

I looked at her and said, "Don't you even feel bad for what you do?"

She was tying her army boots. "No. Feeling sorry is for wimps."

"What's wrong with you? I thought you'd be different. I thought we could live together as sisters but sisters don't steal from each other."

"Where the hell've you been? Sisters in the foster homes steal all the time."

"It's not normal."

"You're not normal," she said.

"I'm more normal than you."

"How many girls take care of their daddy? It's like you're married or something."

At that I slapped her face. Something made me do it. I watched her face change from just a plain face to a hard face in a second and then her hand flew out and she punched me in the stomach.

The wind was knocked out of me and I fell on the bed trying to breathe. Dad came up right then. "What's wrong?" he asked.

Then he turned to Justine. "What did you do?"

"Just hit her to pay her back for slapping me."

"Jesus Christ, you get downstairs."

I got my breath back and turned around to see her raise her third finger to Dad. And she did it like she was used to it. He didn't see. After she snapped her jacket, she grabbed her duffel bag and headed down the stairs.

"Hold that dog," said the sheriff.

I grabbed Buster's collar for a second, then I let go. I liked seeing her scream and jump back, hugging her arms around her, while Buster pushed his snout between her legs. The sheriff grabbed hold of his collar and held him while Justine jumped into the driver's side of the car.

I watched her sit there staring straight ahead. Dad was talking to the sheriff. I thought they were talking about Justine and her rotten ways but then I heard him say something to Dad about planting corn. The sheriff had a patch of land at the beginning of the river road where he played at farming.

The sheriff got in his car and started it. Justine didn't even look at me but kept twirling that hair and staring ahead.

I didn't even wave either.

Buster took off barking at the car, nipping at the tires as it left our lane. Dad came over to the front step. I was cold in my bathrobe so I hurried inside and stood at the front window. Dad came in and stood at the other window.

I was crying.

"What's wrong?" he asked.

"You know," I said.

"What?"

"I wanted it to work out, but I didn't think she'd be like that."

"Yah, she's a wild one. I'd hate to see her when she's your age. God, she'll probably be doing armed robberies by then."

"Don't."

"Don't what?"

"Don't make fun of her. She's screwed up. Next year I plan on studying about her and finding out what's wrong with her."

"You don't need college to do that," he snorted. "Just look

to her folks."

I could hear it coming and I didn't want to hear right now. Not anymore. "Dad, just stop."

"Why do I have to stop? It's true. How do you get a screwed-up kid? Take a drunken whore for a mother and a spic carnie guy for a dad, and that's how you get someone like her."

"Her name's Justine."

"I know what the hell her name is." And Dad turned away from the living room window and went to the kitchen. I heard him rinsing out the coffee pot.

At that I slipped my feet in my tennis shoes, grabbed my jacket from the back of the chair and threw it over my robe and went outside. I didn't know what I was doing or where I was going but I just needed to be away from Dad.

Buster followed me as I walked out the lane and turned south. I had wanted it to work out. I had planned how we would cook together and wash windows and cut out sugar cookies together. It should have worked out. If I had had time, I could have turned her around but I didn't even get a chance to begin. But why did she come here? That was what I couldn't figure out. Why would she come all the way from Florida on a bus to take some nail polish and a picture of Mom? It didn't make sense.

I heard a truck and walked to the side of the gravel road so it could pass. It was Elmer and he honked and slowed down. I heard him stop and the pickup backing up. I walked faster.

"Looks like you just got out of bed," Elmer said.

"Nope, been up an hour," I said.

"Doing your morning exercise?"

"Yup, something like that."

"Strange get-up for exercising."

"It's what I had on."

"You okay?" he asked.

"I'm okay, Elmer. Just go on." And I took off jogging so I could get away from him.

I heard his truck move ahead and gather up speed.

When I got past the Fogarty place, I heard another truck behind me.

It was Dad in our truck. He stopped it a few yards ahead of me and Buster took off and jumped in the back. Traitor dog.

Dad leaned over and rolled down the window. "You won't get very far in that get-up," he said.

"I'll get as far as I want."

"Elmer said you were walking and I said you were upstairs. I didn't think you'd do something dumb like your sis—."

I didn't answer.

"You getting in?"

"Nope."

"You gonna walk to town with that on?"

"Just might," I said.

I began jogging and he kept up with me. Then I turned around and headed back. At that he backed up the truck and stayed with me. And then I turned again and headed toward Emmetsburg.

"How long you gonna keep this up?"

"Don't know."

"Well, a car's coming up ahead." He pointed ahead of us.

"Maybe I'll hitch a ride with them."

"Don't you dare. Get in here right now."

"Nope."

Dad shook his head. The car was getting closer and I knew that he was thinking about what the neighbors would think. He stopped the pickup. Then he said something I didn't expect. "What can I do to get you to change your mind?"

"Say you're sorry about all those things you said about her, about them."

"But they're true."

"I know that, but you don't have to keep harping on them."

"Did you want to leave with your sister? Is that it?"

"No, I didn't say that."

"Maybe you can walk a little faster and catch up with her. Then you two can go find her and live with her." My dad's voice cracked and he had a pained expression on his face.

"Knock it off. I didn't say that."

The car slowed down and looked like it was going to stop. "Jesus, just get in here," Dad said. The farmer in the car looked and Dad gave him an index-finger wave. The car sped on.

"You say you're sorry."

"What am I sorry for?" he exploded, hitting the steering wheel. "Am I sorry I raised you and worked my ass off to support you? Is that what I'm supposed to be sorry for?" His voice was loud. "God dammit, am I sorry for being a dad? Is that what you want?" I saw spit hit the windshield.

"Why do you do this?" I was crying.

"What do you mean?"

"You know, you turn the thing on me. You turn it back to I don't appreciate you. I didn't even bring that up. I was talking about my mom who's a sick lady. We know she's sick and we know now that Justine's kind of sick too."

"So?"

"So … it's just … when you talk about how bad they are I feel like you're saying I'm bad too. And I think you think maybe my birth caused her drinking." I sniffed the snot up into my nose and wiped it on the sleeve of my bathrobe.

Dad pulled a blue bandana out of his pocket and stretched himself to pass it out the window to me. I took it and blew my nose. I was tired of walking. I was tired of talking and I wanted to go home and get in my bed.

"Brigid, I don't mean …" Dad stopped.

"What?" I said. I opened the door of the pickup and stood on the gravel. Buster had moved to the front of the cab and was trying to lick me.

He shook his head and looked away.

"What?" I screamed. "Just what are you saying?"

"I mean …," he paused. "I just don't want you to leave."

There was silence.

I didn't know what to say to that so I just got in the pickup and sat there. Then Dad reached for his handkerchief in my hand and blew his nose. It was a loud blow.

He turned the pickup around in J.B. Bruning's field lane and we headed home. Everywhere I looked I saw plowed fields, dark and expectant, waiting to be planted. Things would start growing again— soon the fields would have life. They'd be fresh and green. Would that happen to me when I left the river road and my dad? Would I be rootless without my dad around or would I be replanted in another place? I just might be like the seed of corn; I might take hold in a new field and burst forth emerging into something silky and golden and desired. Deep within me were the pictures of growth that I saw every spring, and I knew despite heavy rain, hail, and high winds, those plants of corn made it to fall, and I guess I might too.

Acknowledgments

I'm grateful to New Rivers Press Senior Editor Alan Davis, Managing Editor Donna Carlson, and to *The River Road* book team at Minnesota State University Moorhead for making this process an enjoyable one.

I'm forever thankful for my writing group—Jeanne Emmons, Steven Coyne, Deb Freese, Marlene VanderWiel, NancyBraun —and my colleagues in the Briar Cliff English department, especially Phil Hey who gave me encouragement and feedback. I am grateful for my friends who kept me going— Mary Stoltman, Pat Luth Gunia, Colleen Sernett-Shadle, Lee Krause Corbett, Cecil Ogle, Kris Bengford, Lee Kurtz, Jenna Blum, Cornelia Maddelena Hoberg, Carolyn Dinges Guhin, Kitty Foy McDonald, and my sisters and brothers and in-laws—Paul, Sheila, Jim, Phyllis, Rose, Richard, Emmett, Sandy, Mary, Nancy, Pete, Clem, Phillip, Linda, Marty, and Barb.

And most of all I'd like to thank my family—my husband Bob and my children—Rachel, Colin, and Alison Currans-Sheehan, and my son-in-law Nathan Henry.

I gratefully acknowledge the following publications where some of the stories in this collection first appeared:

"The Last Trapshoot" in *The Virginia Quarterly Review*, Summer 2000, and in *The Egg Lady and Other Neighbors* (New Rivers Press), 2004.

"Robert Emmet Rides Again" in *Connecticut Review*, Winter 2003-2004.

"The Cockfight" in *South Dakota Review*, Spring 2002.

"The Fogartys of the River Road" in *Rainbow Curve*, Issue 6, Spring 2005.

"Hitting the Bull's-eye" is forthcoming in *13th Moon*.

Biography

Tricia (Patricia) Currans-Sheehan is a native of Emmetsburg, Iowa. The ninth of ten children born to Salome Antoine and James Henry Currans, she grew up on a 280-acre farm on the river road between Emmetsburg and Graettinger. She attended the Catholic schools in Emmetsburg until the closing of the high school, graduating from Graettinger Community School. She received her B.A. in English from Briar Cliff College and her M.A. and Ph.D. from the University of South Dakota. In 1980 she began teaching at Briar Cliff University and founded The *Briar Cliff Review,* a literary arts magazine, in 1988. Her work has been published in *Fiction, Frontiers, Virginia Quarterly Review, Puerto del Sol, CALYX, Connecticut Review,* and many other journals. She lives in Sioux City, Iowa, with her husband Bob, and has three children: Rachel, Colin, and Alison Currans-Sheehan.